Ben Preston

Dialect

And other Poems

Ben Preston

Dialect
And other Poems

ISBN/EAN: 9783337158262

Printed in Europe, USA, Canada, Australia, Japan

Cover: Foto ©Andreas Hilbeck / pixelio.de

More available books at **www.hansebooks.com**

BEN PRESTON'S POEMS.

Dialect and other Poems.

BY

BEN PRESTON.

WITH GLOSSARY OF THE LOCAL WORDS.

LONDON:
SIMPKIN, MARSHALL & CO.
BRADFORD: T. BREAR, KIRKGATE.
—
1881.

TO

THOMAS THORNTON EMPSALL, Esq.,

President of the Bradford Historical and Antiquarian Society,

A TRIED AND HELPFUL FRIEND,

THIS BOOK IS RESPECTFULLY DEDICATED BY HIS

OBLIGED AND GRATEFUL WELL-WISHER,

THE AUTHOR.

ADVERTISEMENT.

To meet a growing inquiry for the author's Poetical Works, the publisher made arrangements with him for the issue of a complete Edition, with his own final alterations or corrections. Most of the Dialect Poems have been long out of print, although several Editions have been issued of some at different times. Several of the other Poems possess great merit, but are little known. All that the author cares to preserve are now brought together from every known source for the first time, and have had the full benefit of his own revision, and it is hoped the volume will meet with a generous reception from the reading public. The Portrait is an excellent likeness from a photograph taken expressly for this edition, a few weeks ago, by Mr. E. J. Passingham, of Bradford.

BRADFORD, *Dec.*, 1880.

PREFACE.

An author, on his first appearance in public, often feels called upon to say something about himself or his works. If the said author is a Minor Bard, whose effusions are on the wrong side of mediocrity, he commonly strives to blunt the edge of criticism by statements and excuses little calculated to attain his end.

One of the tribe, for instance, informs his reader that the book before him is the production of a working man who has found amusement for his leisure hours in composing the rhymes it contains, but fails to show why things written for mere amusement should be brought before the public as something worthy of its regard. Another humbly tells the critics that he has had no education, and on that ground pleads for a moderate and merciful flagellation.

The author of the following Dialect and Other Poems is no way disposed to tread in the footprints of his predecessors. He might, if he chose, inform his readers that he, too, was a working man, notwithstanding all that his enemies have insinuated to the contrary, but that would be but a poor excuse for parading indifferent work. Nor would it much avail him to plead that he was uneducated, for genius, apart from education, can achieve much, while education without genius can never be more than a good copyist. The locomotive of the illiterate Stephenson was a sublime success, whereas the match-tax of the polished and classical Lowe was an infamous failure. The first is the admiration of philosophers, the second, the derision of street Arabs.

On the merits or defects of the accompanying productions the author ventures to give no opinion; they will fall into the hands of unbiassed judges, whose estimate will, no doubt, be expressed in their own way. The entire series has been the spontaneous outcome of events and circumstances extending over a lengthened period, and though most of the pieces have lain in undisturbed repose in the ephemeral literature of the time, several have been in circulation many years, attended by sundry tokens of appreciation. Beyond their origin, however, the author has had little concern in the production or distribution of any of them, and their collected issue now is in no way prompted by his vanity or wishes.

Is this work, then, brought out "in compliance with the solicitation of friends"? Sir and madam, yes. The author affirms the fact in this solemn manner because some may feel a difficulty in believing it, unless the declaration be made, as it were, on oath.   But neither the solicitation of friends, nor the certainty of undying fame which the bard, above all others, is supposed to thirst for, would have induced the author to battle with the difficulties attendant on the collection of these scattered and hidden rhymes.

If, therefore, in Bradford or elsewhere, there are persons who can find a pleasure in the perusal of this book their thanks are due to Mr. Empsall, by whose patient labours most of the pieces have been dug up out of various sepulchres in which, for more than a quarter of a century, they have been quietly inurned.

B. PRESTON.

HAMMONDALE HOUSE,
    November, 1880.

CONTENTS.

NATTERIN' NAN.

NOA daht ye'll all hev ceard abaht
   T'Apollo Belvedere,
A statty thowt by some to be
   Fro' iv'ry failin' tlear.

All reyt an' streyt i' mak' an' shap',
   A mould for t'race o' men :
A dahnreyt, upreyt, beng-up chap,
   Nut mich unlike mysen.

Nah, thau ye knaw he's nowt bud stoan,
   He looks soa grand an' big,
That little durst yo' pool his noas,
   Ur lug his twisted wig.

Pratly, reyt pratly ovver t'floor
   A tip-o'-toas ye walk,
An' hod your breeath for varry awe,
   An' whisper when yo' talk.

Theer's that abaht him—bud I knawn't
   Nut reytly hah to say't—
That mak's yo' feel as small as thieves
   Anent a magistraat.

B

Ye've seen that dolt o' mucky clay
    On t'face o' Pudsa Doas;
T'owd madlin's worn it all his life,
    An' fancied it a noas.

Yond props is like a pair o' tengs
    O' Sykes's, yit, by t'megs,
When he wor sowber as a judge
    I've eeard him call 'em legs.

So Heaven be praised for self-consate;
    Without it, ah sud say,
We'se hate wursen wi' all wur meet
    For ivver an' a day.

When wasters lewks at t'marble god,
    Egoy! hah wide they gape,
An' wonder which they faver t'moast—
    A boggard or an ape.

An' some wi' envy an' wi' spite
    Get filled to that degree
They'd knock his noas off, if they durst,
    Or give him a black ee.

He somehah kests a leet on things
    'At fowk noan wants to see;
There's few likes tellin' what they are,
    Ur what they owt to be.

Wah, wah, perfection nivver did
    To Adam's barns beleng;
An' lewk at mortals when we will,
    We'se fynd a summat wreng.

Owd Adam gate so mesht wi' t'fall
   That all o' t'human race
Grows sadly aht o' shap' i' t'mind,
   I' t'karkiss, an' i' t'face.

Theer's noan so blynd bud they can see
   A fawt i' other men;
I've sometimes met wi' fowk 'at thowt
   They saw one i' thersen.

An' t'best o' chaps al fynd thersen
   At times i' t'fawty class;
I've doubled t'neiv afoar to-day
   At t'fooil i' t'seemin' dlass.

Bud t'warst o' fawts 'at I've seen yit,
   I' woman or i' man,
Is t'weary, naguein', nengin' turn
   'At plagued poor Natterin' Nan.

I went one summer afternooin
   To see her poor old man,
An' 'ardly hed I darkened t'door,
   When t'wurrit thus began :

"Eh! wah! did ivver! what a treat
   To see thy father's son;
Come forrad, lad, an' sit tha dahn,
   An' al set t'kettle on."

"Nay, nay," ah says, " I'm noan o' thame
   'At calls at t'time by t'clock,
An' bumps 'em dahn i' t'corner chair,
   An' gloars reyt hard at t'jock."

"Tha nontcate, witta hod thy tongue?
   He'll sooin be here I think,
Soa, if tha'll sit an' leet thy pipe,
   Ah'll fotch a soap o' drink."

"Owd lass," says I, "tha'rt hey i' boan,
   An' rayther low i' beef."
"Hay, larn," says shoo, "this year or two
   I've hed a deal o' grief.

"Ah'm nut a woman 'at oft speyks,
   Or sings fowk doleful sengs,
Bud I can tell my mind to thee,
   Tha knaws what things belengs.

"Tha's noaticed I noan lewkt so staat,
   An' I can trewly say,
Fro' t'last back end o' t'year to nah
   I've nut been weel a day.

"An' whot wi' sickness, whot wi' grief,
   I'm doin tha may depend—
It's been a weary mooild an' tew,
   Bud nah it gets near t'end.

"Ah've bowt all t'sister 'at I hev
   A black merrinah gahn;
Fowk thinks I'm rarely off, bud, lad,
   I'm thenkful 'at I'm bahn.

"Wi' t'world, an' ivverything 'at's in't,
   I'm crossed to that degree
That monny a time i' t'day I've prayed
   To lig me down an' dee.

" Whot I've to tak' fro' t'least i' t'hahse
    Is moar nur flesh can bear;
  It isn't just a time by chonce,
    Bud ivvery day i' t'year.

" Noa livin' sowl atop o' t'earth
    Wor tried as I've been tried;
  There's noab'dy bud the Lord an' me
    'At knaws what I've to bide.

" Fro' t'wind i' t'stomach, t'rheumetism,
    An' tengin pains i' t'goom,
  Fro' coughs an' cowds an' t'spine i' t'back,
    I've suffered martyrdom.

" Bud noab'dy pities ma ur thinks
    I'm ailin' owt at all;
  T'poar slave mun tug an' tew wi' t'wark
    Whol ivver shoo can crawl.

" An' Johnny's t'moast unfeelin' brewt
    'At ivver ware a heead:
  He woddant weg a hand ur fooit
    If I wor all bud deead.

" I' t'midst o' all I've hed to due
    That roag wor nivver t'man
  To fotch a coil, ur scar a fleg,
    Ur wesh a pot ur pan.

" Fowk says ahr Sal al sooin be wed,
    Bud t'thowts on't turns ma sick;
  I'd rayther hing her up by t'neck,
    Ur see her berrid wick.

" An' if I thowt a barn o' mine
    Wor born to lead my life,
I suddant think it wor a sin
    To stick her wi' my knife.

" I've axed ahr Johnny twenty times
    To bring a sweep to t'door;
Bud nah afoar I'll speyk ageean
    I'll sit i' t'hahse an' smooar.

" An' then—gooid gracious, what a wind
    Comes whewin thru t'doar sneck;
I felt it all t'last winter, like
    A whittle at my neck.

" That sink-pipe, too, gate stopt wi' muck
    Aboon a fortnit sin',
So ivvery ahr i' t'day wi' t'slops
    I'm treshin' aht an' in.

" Aw! when I think hah I've been tret,
    An' hah I tew an' strive—
To tell tha t'honist trewth, I'm capt
    To fynd myseln alive.

" When he's been rakin' aht o' t'neet,
    At t'markit or at t'fair,
Sich thowts hes come into my cead
    As lifted up my hair.

" I've thowt ' Ay, lad, when tha comes hoam,
    Tha'll fynd ma hung by t'neck;'
An' then I've mebbe thowt ageean
    'At t'cooard 'ud happen breck.

" Ur else I've muttered, ' If it worn't
   So dark, an' cowd, an' weet,
I'd go to t'navvy or to t'dam
   An' drahnd myseln to-neet.'

" It's grief, lad, nowt at all bud grief,
   'At wastes ma day by day ;
So Sattan temps ma, 'cos I'm wake,
   To put myseln away."

T'owd chap eeard pairt o' what shoo said
   As he com' clompin' in,
An' shaated in a red-faced rage,
   " Od, rot it ! hod thy din."

Then Nan began to froth an' fume,
   An' fizz like bottled drink ;
" What, then, tha's entered t'hahse ageean,
   Tha offald-lewkin slink !

" Tha nivver comes thease doors within
   Bud tha mun curse an' sweear,
An' strive to bring ma to my grave
   Wi' breedin' hurries here.

" Fro' thee an' thine sin' wed we wor
   I've taen no end o' grief,
An' nah tha stamps ma under t'fooit,
   Tha murderin' roag an' thief.

" Tha villain, gie ma whot I browt
   That day 'at we wor wed,
An' nivver moar wi' one like thee
   Will I set fooit i' bed."

Here t'dowdy lifted tuv her een
    A yird o' linen check,
An' sobbed an' roared and rockt hersen,
    As if her heart 'ud breck.

An' then shoo rave reyt up by t'rooits
    A handful of her hair,
An' fittered like a deein duck,
    An' shuttered aht o' t'chair.

"Aw! Johnny, run for t'doctor, lad,
    I feel I can't tell hah;"
Says Johnny, "Leet thy pipe ageean,
    Shoo'll coom abaht enah."

Says I, "I nivver saw a chap
    So ceasyful an' fat;
Tha'll suarly len' a helpin' hand
    To lift her off o' t'plat."

Bud better hed it been for him
    If he'd ne'er sturred a peg;
My garters! what a pawse he gat
    Fro' Nan's rheumatic leg.

Sooin, varry sooin, shoo coom abaht,
    An' flung an' tare an' rave,
I' sich a way as fchw could due
    Wi' one fooit i' ther grave.

Then at it went her tongue ageean
    That minnit shoo gat cease,
"Tha villain, tha, tha knaws thy ways
    Brings on sich girds as theease.

"Aw! if tha'd strike ma stiff at once,
　　Ur stab ma to my heart,
　I then could dee content, for fowk
　　Wod knaw reyt what ta art.

"Unfeelin' brewt! unfeelin' brewt!
　　I neer wor weel an' strong;
　Theer's nobbud one thing cheers ma nah—
　　I cannot last so long.

"To stand up for a thing 'at's reyt
　　It isn't i' my nater;
　Theer's fowk 'at knaws I awlus wor
　　A poor, soft, quiat crater.

"One thing I can say, if to-neet
　　My life sud end its leease,
　I've doin my duty, an' tha knaws
　　I've awlus striven for peeace.

"I knaw, I knaw, 'at I'm i' t'gate—
　　Thah's other oats to thresh,
　So, when I'm doin for, tha may wed
　　Yond gooid-for-nowt young tresh."

Then Nan pooled summat aht o' t'drawer,
　　White as a summer claad,
　Says I to Johnny, "What's that theer?"
　　Says Johnny, "It's a shraad.

"An' t'coffin coom tue, bud I sware
　　I wodant ha't i' t'hahse;
　So when shoo's muled shoo sews at that,
　　As quiat as a mahse."

Poor Nan lewkt at me wi' a lewk
  So yonderly an' sad:
"Tha'll come to t'berrin?" "Yis," I said,
  "I sal be varry dlad."

"Then bid thy mother," Johnny cried,
  "An' ax thy Uncle Ben;
An' all her prayers for suddan deeath
  Sal hev my best 'Amen.'"

T'SHORT-TIMER.

IT wor misty an' frosty an' dark as a booit,
  An' soa cowd ye'd ha'e pitied a toad,
When ah eeard to me thinkin' a leet little fooit
  Pit-pattin' behint ma on t'road.

Nah, at five ur awf-past, ov a cowd winter morn,
  Ah'd noa thowts ov a cumrade at all,
So ah stude whol thear coom up a bit ov a barn,
  Like a peggy-stick airin' a shawl.

"Hollou, lass," ah said, as I tapt hur o' t'crahn,
  "Tha'll be doin for i' t'river ur t'kiln;
Whot are ta, yo' monkey, an' wheer are ta bahn?"
  Says shoo, "A short-timer to t'miln."

"If that maister o' thine's onny childer," ah said,
  "Ah sud like 'em to march at thy back;
Bud, ah guess, if tha'd laid an ahr longur i' bed
  'At trade 'ud begin to be slack."

"Hay! maister," shoo said, "ah've eeard t'governer sweear
  'At he's made nowt by t'trade for this age,
An' his horses an' carriages nips him so bare
  Whol he 'ardly can thoil to gie wage.

" Then he's bowt an istaat, an' he's beeldin' a hahse,
    Ey ! an' t'cost on't no mortal knaws yit ;
If we pinch whol wer cubbords weant paster a mahse
    He can nobbud just stand on his fit.

" He says furriners latly hes made a gurt spring,
    An' they live on chopt cabbage an' snam ;
Soa it hoins him, ye see, to shut brass like a king,
    An' then sell i' t'same markets wi' thame.

" If we doan't work for little, we moant work at all,
    An' my gronfathur said yusterneet
If it worn't for t'short-timers 'at t'systum 'ud fall,
    An' t'plewshare cum back into t'street."

Ah lewkt off t'ee-end 'at that wizand owd barn,
    An' ah said, " It appears like to me
'At t'factory an' t'mansion an' t'main o' t'consarn
    Is uphodden by midges like thee."

Here ah pairted wi' t'barn, an' ah cuddant bud laugh,
    Thau ah felt noan so mich at my eease,
For ah thowt to myseln—it's a bonny come-off
    If we're propt by sich pillars as theease.

OWD MALLY.

IN a one-storey, aht-o'-t'way, tumal-dahn cot
   Poor owd Mally sate mournin' her desolate lot,
For of all 'at once awned her nut one wor o' t'spot
    To befriend her i' t'time of her need.
Shoo'd a husband 'at wrowt on t'heeway breckin stoan,
An' when life left his frame it left little bud boan,
An' shoo once hed two dowters, bud nah shoo's aloan,
    For boath dowters an' t'gronchilder deed.

An' shoo once had a lad, sich a prince of a lad !
Bud when t'lass 'at he worshipt gat wed he went mad,
Tuke to drinkin' an' powchin, an' all 'at wor bad,
    An' shoo's eeard nowt abaht him for years;
So owd Mally sits knittin' thru t'midsummer ceats,
Thinkin' sadly o' thame 'at once filled t'empty seeats;
Bud it isn't for t'deead, it's for t'livin' shoo freeats—
    It's for t'lad 'at shoo's droppin' them tears.

Theer's no peeass for her mind, for by day an' by neet
Shoo's a prey to some fancy 'at gives her a freet;
If shoo knew he wor deead an' at rest aht o' t'seet,
    Shoo'd fynd rest for herseln in a while;
Bud shoo's flayed he's i' prison, or sickly, or poor,
Beggin' crusts an' cowd wotter at Charity's doar,
Or else sinkin' i' folly an' sin moar an' moar,
    Growin' viler fro' contact wi' t'vile.

It's a mercy wer feelin's gets blunted an' numb,
As we draw near to t'spot wheer no sorra can come ;
So i' t'end t'poor owd lass gav' up lewkin so dlum,
    An' her grief sattled dahn tuv a calm ;
Thau for Mally no sunshine made breet this dull earth,
Yit a peeass filled her sowl 'at wor better nur mirth,
Sich an eemin as hers seemed to speyk of the birth
    Of a morn full of dlory an' balm.

Thau shoo clamm'd nah an' then, wor ill-clad an' ill-shod,
Thau her portion seemed mainly affliction an' t'rod,
Yit i' t'midst on't theer grew a strong faith in her God
    An' a comfortin' trust in His word.
" Yis, I'm feeble," shoo said, " bud wi' help I sal stand,
I'm i' t'dark, bud I knaw 'at Tha'll leead ma by t'hand,
An' wheerivver yond lad be, on sea or on land,
    He'll be safe i' Thy keepin', O Lord."

Well, i' t'end a lame sowjer, weel blackened wi' t'sun,
Com' to Mally's an' browt her rare news of her son—
" Like a hero yahr Timothy stude to his gun,
    An' he fell shaatin ' Hip, hip, hurrah ' ! "
" Did he dee wheer he fell ? "   " Nay, we ran to his aid,
An' i' t'hospital moar nur a fortnit he laid,
An' then, claspin' his hands, for his comrades he prayed,
    An' wi' praise on his lips passed away."

Poor owd Mally we called her, bud nivver no moar
Let a mortal man say 'at owd Mally is poor,
For wi' joy an' thenksgivin her heart's runnin' o'er,
    An' shoo's oft singin' aht, " Hip, hurrah ! "
Hip, hurrah ! hip, hurrah ! them wor t'words of her son,
As he fell like a hero aside of his gun ;
Bud shoo thinks o' no vict'ry bud that 'at wor won
    When his sowl passed in triumph away.

COME TO THY GRONNY, DOY.

COME to thy gronny, doy, come to thy gronny,
    Bless tha, to me tha'rt as pratty as onny;
Mutherlass barn of a dowter unwed,
Little tha knaws, doy, the tears 'at I've shed;
Trials I've knawn boath for t'heart an' for t'heead,
Shortnass o' wark, ey, an' shortnass o' breead.

Thease I could bide, bud thau tha'rt noan to blame,
Bless tha, tha browt ma boath sorra an' shame;
Gronny, poar sowl, for a two month ur moar
Hardly could feshun to lewk aht o' t'doar;
T'nabors called aht to me, " Dunnot stand that,
Aht wi' that hussy an' aht wi' her brat."

Deary me, deary me, what could I say?
T'furst thing of all I thowt—let ma go pray;
T'next time I slept I'd a dream, d'ye see,
Ey! an' I knew 'at that dream wor for me—
Tears of Christ Jesus, I saw 'em that neet,
Fall drop by drop on to one at His feet.

After that, saw Him wi' barns rahnd His knee,
Some on 'em, happen, poar craters like thee;
Says I at last, though I soarly wor tried,
Suarly a sinner, a sinner sud bide;
Nabors may think or may say what they will,
T'mother an' t'dowter sal stop wi' ma still.

Come on't what will, i' my cot they sal cahr,
Woe be to them 'at maks bad into wahr:
Some fowk may call tha a name 'at I hate,
Wishin' fro' t'heart tha wor weel aht o' t'gate,
Oft this hard world into t'gutter al shuv tha,
Poar little lamb, wi' no daddy to love tha.

Dunnot thee freeat, doy, whol gronny hods up,
Nivver sal tha want a bite or a sup;
What if I work thease owd fingurs to t'boan,
Happen tha'll love ma long after I'm goan;
T'last bite i' t'cubbord wi' thee I could share't,
Hay! bud tha's stown a rare slice o' my heart.

Spite ov all t'sorra, all t'shame 'at I've seen,
Sunshine comes back to my heart thru thy een;
Cuddle thy gronny, doy,
Bless tha, tha'rt bonny, doy,
Rosy an' sweet fro' thy brah to thy feet,
Kingdoms an' crahns wodn't buy tha to-neet.

AH NIVVER CAN CALL HER MY WIFE.

AH'M a weyver, ye knaw, an' awf decad,
    So ah due all 'at ivver ah can
To put away aht o' my ecad
    The thowts an' the aims of a man.
Eight shillin' i' t'wick's what ah arn
    When ah've varry gooid wark an' full time,
An' ah think it's a sorry consarn
    For a fellah 'at's just in his prime.

Bud ahr maister says things is as well
    As they have been or ivver can be,
An' ah happen sud think so mysel'
    If he'd nobbud swop places wi' me.
Bud he's welcome to all he can get,
    Ah begrudge him o' noan ov his brass,
An' ah'm nowt bud a madlin to fret,
    Ur to think o' yond bewtiful lass.

Ah nivver can call her my wife,
    My love ah sal nivver mak' knawn,
Yit the sorra that darkens her life
    Thraws its shadda across o' my awn.
When ah knaw 'at her heart is at eease,
    Theer is sunshine an' singin' i' mine;
An' misfortunes may come as they pleease,
    Yit they seldom can mak' ma repine.

C

Bud that Chartist wor nowt bud a sloap—
  Ah wor fooild by his speeches an' rhymes,
For his promises wottered my hoap,
  An' ah leng'd for his sunshiny times;
Bud I feel 'at my dearest desire
  Within ma al wither away,
Like an ivy-stem trailin' i' t'mire
  It's deein for t'want of a stay.

When ah laid i' my bed day an' neet,
  An' wor geen up by t'doctors for deead,
God bless her! shoo'd com' wi' a leet
  An' a basin o' grewil an' breead.
An' ah once thowt ah'd aht wi' it all,
  Bud soa kindly shoo chatted an' smiled,
Ah wor fain to turn ovver to t'wall,
  An' to bluther an' roar like a child.

An' ah said, as I thowt of her een,
  Each breeter for t'tear 'at wor in't,
It's a sin to be nivver forgeen,
  To yoke her to famine an' stint;
So ah'll een travel forrad throo life,
  Like a man throo a desert unknawn;
Ah mun neer hev a hoam nur a wife,
  Bud my sorras al all be my awn.

Soa ah trudge on aloan as ah owt,
  An' whotivver my troubles may be,
They'll be sweetened, poor lass, wi' the thowt
  'At I've nivver browt trouble to thee.
Yit a burd hes its young uns to guard,
  A wild beast a mate in his den,
An' ah cannot bud think 'at it's hard—
  Nay, deng it, ah'm roarin' agen.

UNCLE BEN.

THEAR'S men 'at al treyd upo' women an' barns
   In a mad-ceaded scrammal for brass,
An' begrudge a poor chap what he 'onistly aarns,
   If he's seen wi' his pipe an' his dlass.

Theer's men 'at al gobble up all they can get,
   An' al spare nut a morsil for t'poar ;
An' thear's sum 'at al feeast boath thersen an' ther set—
   Ey ! if t'bailies be standin' at t'door.

Thear's boan-idle nowbles, baht hahses an' lands,
   'At al walk on a carpeted path,
An' nivver due nowt wi' ther lily-white hands
   Bud lift uther fowk's jock to ther maath.

Sum al pine ther awn mothers, pop trahzuz an' coit,
   An' then drink what 'ud fill a draw-well,
Nivver thinkin' 'at t'thirst 'at they feel i'ther throit
   Is a cowk 'at wor lected i' hell.

Bud away wi' sich fellahs, we'll name 'em no moar,
   Bud we'll turn tuv a model for men ;
For the chap to be copied by rich an' by poar
   Is my 'ard-workin', brave Uncle Ben.

Whotivver he hannals is honistly won ;
   In his words an' his actions he's trew ;
He nivver saw t'face ov a bill or a dun,
   For he pays i' 'ard brass what is due.

He rises at six, an' he's off tuv his wark,
   An' thru t'day he's as threng as a bee ;
An' as suar as a gun, when it gets to be dark,
   He'll be sittin' wi' t'wife at his tea.

Then he'll rowl upo' t'hearth-rug wi' Harry an' Will,
   Like a cat wi' her kittens at play ;
Ur sit throaned i' his chair wi' his pipe an' his gill,
   An' to Nell read the news o' the day.

He's awlus moar ready to pity nur blame
   The failin's o' women an' men,
An' oft for ther fawts an excuse he can frame,
   When they cannot frame one for thersen.

Hurrah for rare Ben an' his innacent life !
   A better lad nivver wor knawn !
He delights in his barns, an' theer's noabody's wife
   'At he likes awf as weel as his awn.

God bless that owd joiner, his basket an' hoam,
   An' God bless his wife an' his breed ;
For if ivver fro t'fireside he's tempted to roam,
   It's to help a poor chap in his need.

T'SACRED DRAWER.

BY t'dim red leet of a sinkin' sun,
  'Tenderly, tenderly, one by one
Shoo laid aht her treasures o' t'chamer flooar;
  Thrustin' her face into t'cloas o' t'bed,
  "All on um, all on um's theer," shoo said,
"Bud my Johnny—Ah nivver mun lewk on moar."

Scattered abaht o' that chamer flooar,
  Lakuns an' little duds theer they wor,
Sad upkessen bits of a sucken wreck;
  Baa-lam', an' trumpet, an' top, an' ball,
  Still as if t'deeath-stroke 'ad smitten all;
Poor thing, ye'd ha' thowt at her heart 'ud breck.

Put by his lakuns, his tloas repack—
  Nivver no mooar will Johnny come back,
For he cares nowt nah for what pleased him t'best;
  T'eaglet, when makkin' his skyward spring,
  Scatters wi' t'waff of his mighty wing
All t'feathers an' t'fur 'at hed lined his nest.

Under his hat as it ligs o' t'flooar,
  Summat shoo sees 'at shoo's seen afoar,
An' it fassens her een in a dreamy stare;
  Sunbeams 'at breetened a by-goan day,
  Breezes 'at long sin hes passed away—
They're tontlin' wi' t'curls of his gowlden hair.

Music an' sunshine, an' birds an' flaars,
  Gladden like playmates them few short haars
'At ivver he spent aht o' t'hives o' men.
    Poor little chap, hah he sammd 'em up,
    Blue-bell, an' daisy, an' gowlden cup;
Bud noan i' all t'field 'at could match hissen.

    Suddenly, sharply, wi' gasp an' start,
    Back comes her grief tuv her cheated heart,
To darken her joy like a thunner claad.
    Once mooar shoo sits whol her watch is done,
    Once mooar shoo's weepin' aloan, aloan,
Wi' a snaw-white face an' a snaw-white shraad.

    T'snand's in her ears o' that fallin' tlay;
    T'end comes at last o' that long, long day,
When at midneet shoo lifted her voice an' cried,
    "Husband! aw, husband! ah can't luke up,
    Trouble has drahnded boath faith an' hope,
An' ah cannot turn keigh wi' my barn ahtside.

    "T'flaars he once gethered wi' childish greed
    Faded as he did an' drooped an' deed,
Bud t'Spring called 'em up agean, one by one;
    T'soil on his grave hes been damped wi' tears,
    Spring shaars an' sunbeams hes fallen for years,
Bud Johnny sleeps on, yis, Johnny sleeps on."

    Johnny sleeps long i' that barren tlay,
    Bud his mother hes leearn'd to wait an' pray,
An' her sorra's been changed for a solemn bliss.
    Neet after neet as some good deed's done,
    Dahn from his home comes her little son
An' leaves on her forheead an' angel's kiss.

T'CREAKIN' GAAT.

LONG sin', when me an' t'missis furst
   Set up i' wedded staat,
We'd a near neighbour knawn fur years
   By t'name o' T'Creakin' Gaat.

Ah knew her in her yaathful days—
   A forrad, flawpin' slut,
'At eust to talk an' fooil wi' t'chaps
   Thru t'oppan windah shut.

I think, when ah consither t'pairs
   'At mak's it up to coart,
'At Fate oft tethers t'warst to t'best
   To mak' a middlin' soort.

For, doan't yo' see, if fiend wed fiend,
   An' limbs bred in an' in;
Ah lewkt on't 'at we'se varry sooin
   Be up to t'naff i' sin.

If ivvery divel fan his match,
   Ther seed an' breed, begow!
Wod mak' a hell atop o' t'eearth,
   As ut as that below.

Ye knaw nah hah it coom to pass,
    Thau t'reason fehw hes guessed,
A dowdy like that Creakin' Gaat
    Gat wed to Sammy Best.

A gooid, 'ard-workin', deacent lad
    As ivver bate o' breead;
Poar fellah, he'd a deeal o' heart
    Bud feaful little heead.

Fowk wondered hah soa soft a chap
    Hed cahncild Sarah Slurr;
I'gow, shoo knew no man on earth
    Could be too soft for hur.

Sal's bewty charmed poar silly Sam
    (What baits our hearts ingage),
Sam addled thirty bob i' t'wick,
    An' Sal wor charmed wi' t'wage.

'Twor dark November when they met
    For t'furst time i' ther life;
T'next haliday wor New Year's Day,
    An' they wor man an' wife.

Ay, an' a slarin wife shoo wor,
    As ivver deetud sark,
That ate an' drank o' t'varry best,
    Bud fainted ower hur wark.

Ah'm just as if ah saw hur nah,
    Wi' slippers on for shooin,
A flannil claht abaht hur eead,
    An' t'neetcap on at nooin.

Thear, tlois to t'harstun, cheek to jawm,
  Shoo'd cahr by t'hahr an' snoar,
Wi' t'blenkit ovver t'winter-hedge,
  To keep off t'draught o' t'doar.

An' when shoo tuke a stride ur two,
  Shoo plantud t'neiv o' t'hip,
An' pucker'd up hur faas an' stuck
  Hur teeth i' t'lower lip.

Shoo kept a stock o' queer cumplaints
  As ivver mortal seed,
An' donn'd 'em on an' dofft 'em off,
  Like tloas to suit hur need.

It wor a freet 'at furst browt on
  That pain withaht a naam :
Shoo thinks hur heart's lowpt aht o' t'place,
  An' moar nur hur thinks t'saam.

It adds, ye mind, aboon a bit
  To other pains an' toils,
Bud nowt no sooiner brings it on
  Nur t'thowts o' fotchin t'coils.

Sum thinks 'at fowk 'at eyts like Sal
  Is far moar flayed nur hurt ;
Eh ! barn ! a crater laid on reyt
  Hes need o' some support.

Shoo tew'd, poar sowl, to breeten up,
  An' tried, whotivver coom,
To cook hur chop an' keep hur meeals
  O' summat warm i' t'room.

Poar Sam wor capt shoo grew so fat
    On scarce a bite ur sup ;
Bless yo', them fellahs little knaws
    Hah sorra blaws us up.

One day they fotcht him fro' his wark,
    Thinkin' shoo're bahn to dee,
He saw her fidge wi' hand an' fooit,
    An' turn up t'white o' t'ee.

Whol Sam wor roarin' in theer coom
    A redish-noased owd dame,
'At hinted brandy browt fowk rahnd
    When they'd sich bahts as thame.

An' soa wi' brandy Sarah sooin
    Reyt nicely rahnd wor browt ;
Ah wish t'teetotelers could ha'e seen
    The miracle it rowt.

Bet Bates may fling aht what shoo likes,
    An' girn an' fleer an' scoff,
Bud it's that spooinful twice i' t'day
    'At keeps that colic off.

Once on a time, at six o' t'morn,
    As ivverybody knaws,
Wi' moarnful faas an' joyful heart
    Sal Best went off to t'spaws.

Hur cough wor bad, hur lungs wor doin,
    Hur liver worn away,
An' theer wor fowk 'at thowt an' said
    Shoo'd 'ardly live a day.

Sam roared to see hur, as he thowt,
 Soa worn an' all bud goan,
An' axt a friend to let him knaw
 Hah t'wife wor gettin' on.

When shoo'd been off a wick or soa,
 A letter coom for Sam,
He read it, doubled t'neiv, an' hissed
 What saandud like a "damn."

I' t'deead o' t'neet a broker com',
 An' aht wi' t'traps he twined;
He didn't leave a stick behint
 Exceptin' t'windah blind.

So Sam gat shut o' t'haasel gooids,
 Paid off t'wife's debt for gin,
Then tuke dahn Sloper Loin wi' t'brass,
 An's neer been heeard on sin'.

When Sal com' back shoo gate a keigh,
 Bud when shoo oppened t'doar
Hur hoam hed vanisht, bud shoo fahnd
 A letter laid o' t'flooar.

" Dear wife,—Tha'll feel when tha returns
 A touch o' t'owd cumplaint;
Bud as I've left a penny caak,
 I'se nivver see tha want.

" I've awlus been a tewin chap—
 We've nauther child nur chick,
An' yit, I think tha'll fynd it 'ard
 To carry on a wick.

" Wi' thee, I've wark whol I can work,
    An' t'warkhahse when I can't;
Bud I'm for strivin' to divorce
    That couple, Age an' Want.

" That doncin wi' an officer
    I' t'ball-rahm awf undrest
Proves tha's been diddlin' monny a year
    Thy husband, Sammy Best."

STAND UP, LADS, AN' LET'S HEV
A FEYT.

THEAR'S a decal o' things wrong 'at we mean to mak' reyt,
   So, dal it, stand up, lads, an' let's hev a feyt;
If we stick weel together an' keep up wer pluck,
Like a flee aht o' t'treacle, we'se fidge aht o' t'muck.

Tak' noatis, if irver ye mean to be men,
T'furst battles an' t'hardest al be wi' yersen;
When ye tussle for t'wage just allah ivvry man
For his hoam an' his wife to due t'best 'at he can.

Dunnot strike below t'belt when ye're manfully met,
Auther lick wi' fair feytin' ur tak' tul't ye're bet,
We'se ne'er see mich betterness spring up i' t'land
Wol worker can thoil to tak' worker by t'hand.

Dunnot run after brass whol ye're blawn aht o' breeath,
Nur mak' life wi' unrest like a shuttle i' t'sheeath,
Let yer daywarks be nauther to hard nur to long,
An' yer leisure be sweetened wi' music an' song.

Let's feyt for t'poar mothers 'at addles ther scran
By weyvin' fro' dayleet to dark like a man,
For a hoam lost an' dowly receives 'em at neet—
Ther husbands at t'aleass, ther childer i' t'street.

An' let's feyt for sweet boams an' a sect o' green grass
Aht o' t'stink o' this sewage, an' brimstone, an' gas,
Wheer wer childer, let aht into t'sunshine an' t'air,
May grow graceful i' body, an' healthy, an' fair.

Nut swarmin' i' ginnels awf naykt an' awf rotten,
Bleared imps aht o' t'witches o' Macbeth by Sattan :
" Dreams, dreams," says Old Turncog, " that Ruskin's a flat,"
Bud we've doin devil's wark 'at's as hard as all that.

Is labour an' skill—that's two pairts aht o' t'three—
To be hectored an' diddled by duffers like thee ?
Is a hundred poor fowk to go stinted an' bare
That a fooil may turn aht in a carriage an' pair ?

For wark-fowk i' cellars a grand thing this trade is,
Upheld an' bepraised by all Europe's fine ladies ;
Just nah, when poor France regged an' tattered an' bare is,
We're weyvin' silk lustres for t' harlots i' Paris.

Let trade's blessèd martyr, St. Cobden the Holy,
Sing psalms o' thenksgivin' to Feshion an' Folly ;
We sal lewk up for help to no Parliament men—
They're to threng, ivv'ry one on 'em, helpin' thersen.

For t'changes we're wantin' we willut long wait,
An' ye're axt to due nowt nobbut get aht o' t'gate,
An' if pahr-loom an' spinnal lords says it's no goa
They'll get pawsed aht o' t'mule hoil by Odgers & Co.

T'OWD PSALM TUNE.

SOME cowks warmed my knees wi' ther dull red heat
   When I'd swallud my milk an' pobs,
Soa tlois up to t'fender ah pooled my seeat
   An' ah planted my fit on t'hobs.

Then lectin' my short black pipe, ah swung
   Reyt back i' my owd arm chair,
An' ah sat watchin' t'reek as it raze au' hung
   Like a sperit i' t'midneet air.

Sister Mally au' t'barns wor asleep upstairs—
   Thear wor pecass wi' that blatin' crew—
So ah smoked an' ah thowt o' my wasted years,
   An' o' t'wark 'at wor yit to due.

As ah lewkt at this life an' at t'life to be,
   Ah said to mysen, " Tha ass !
Wi' comfort tha nauther can live nur dee,
   For tha's saved nauther sowl nur brass."

Then spyin' owd Sattan astride o' t'clahd
   'At wor hung under t'chamer flooar,
Ah doubled my neive an' said, " Hark tha, lad,
   Ah'll be diddled wi' thee no mooar;

" If my sins be like leead, an' like cork my purse,
    Wah, thear's noab'dy bud thee to thenk ;
Bud when t'world's a wick owder, tha gernin' curse,.
    I'se her been boath to t'Church an' to t'Benk."

Then some minnits passed ovver me, sad an' dree,
    An' my thowts grew as dark as t'neet,
When some drucken owd hals 'at hed been on t'spree
    Com' singin' like mad up t'street.

Wi' ther hands an' ther fit they kept beatin' t'time
    As ther arms into t'air wor flung,
Ey ! an' t'words of a godless an' silly rhyme
    Tuv an owd psalm tune they sung.

Hay ! the times 'at ah've joined i' that grand owd air,.
    When owd friends at my side wor seen,
When my life wor a sunshiny haliday,
    An' this wizand owd world wor green.

I' t'leet of a sun 'at hes long sin' set
    Ah see t'chapel on Primrose Brah,
An' what friends on a Sabbath day theer hes met
    'At for ivver is pairted nah.

They come an' they smile an' away they pass,
    Bud they awlus leave one i' view—
A poar little fatherless country lass,
    'At once sat i' t'singers' pew.

One calm summer neet as we sang t'last hymn
    Shoo lewkt i' my faas reyt hard ;
An' her lips wor white an' her een wor dim
    When ah joined her i' t'chapel yard.

An' shoo said to ma, "Ben, ah feel faint an' ill,
  Tha mun gic ma thy arm, owd lad;"
An' shoo whispered some words 'at ah think on still,
  For they made ma reyt prahd and dlad.

Soa ah helpt her wi' care ovver rail an' stile,
  Whol we gate tuv her gardin dooar,
Then shoo held ma by t'hand sich a long, long while—
  An' ah saw her alive no moar.

Well, this world gets as cowd an' as hard as steel,
  An' at times ah feel fain shoo's dead,
For shoo'd hard to slave at her loom an' wheel
  For a morsil o' honist breead.

Moar nur twenty year shoo's been dead an' goan,
  Bud wheerivver ma lot may be,
When t'hahse is all wisht an' ah'm left aloan,
  Shoo awlus comes back to me.

Ah've wished 'at ah'd tell'd her by t'gardin dooar
  Hah deep wor my love an' trew,
For her friends, poor lass, they wor fehw an' pooar—
  Bud no matter, ah think shoo knew.

Hay! if ivver ah get to yond place aboon,
  Wheer ah long i' ma heart to be,
Just to hear her once moar sing that owd psalm tune
  Al be heaven of itseln to me.

D

T'LANCASHIRE FAMINE.

"NAY weyver," ah said, "thau ah pity thy doom,
  Ah've a wife an' ten childer i' one little room,
An' t'owd lass, as tha sees, hes another i' t'loom ;
  Ah really can spare nowt to-day."
Soa Lanky turned aht wi' a tear in his ee,
An' he bate his low lip in a way, d'ye see,
'At went like a knife thru ahr Margrit an' me ;
  Lord help him—ah hoap he can pray.

Ah wor tossed like a drunkun man's noddle all t'neet,
For I saw i' my dreams sich a pitiful seet,
Of hahsuz as cowd an' as empty as t'street,
  Wi' little things tlammin' o' t'floor ;
Ah wor roarin' at t'seet on't an' dryin' my noas,
When an angil com up to ma, so ah suppoas,
For he'd wings on his back an' wor donn'd i' white cloas,
  An' they've awlus comed that way afoar.

He lewked at me kindly, an' whispered, "Alas !
Ah know tha't ta poor to gie t'poor onny brass ;
Bud it's thowt up aboon 'at a man o' thy class
  Owt to sing 'em a ditty at least."
"Just the ticket," ah answered, "an' hearken ye, squire,
If ye'll come dahn some eenin' an' sit by my fire,
Ye sal guide as ya like boath ma voice an' ma lyre,
  An' then some'dy 'at's pinin' sal feeast."

Soa t'next ccmin' when t'work-a-day racket wor still,
Ah beckoned him dahn wi' a wave o' my quill,
An' ah shaatud aht, " Michael, we'll frame, if ta will,
    O' that seng 'at tha'rt bahn to inspire."
Bud he said when he com he mud hurry up t'stairs
Wi' a tlois-written bundil o' Pharisees' prayers.
Ah wor capt 'at an angil ud tew wi' sich wares,
    Bud they saved 'em, he said, to leet t'fire.

Says Michael, " Draw pen an' ink sketches ageean
O' yond famishin' bodies, despairin' an' leean,
An' then ax Yorkshur chaps what the engmond they meean
    To wear hearts i' ther bellies like stoans ?
They shine as they're gettin' ther bacca an' ale,
An' drahndin' wi' music yond Lancashire wail,
Whol famine, that wild beast wi' tooith an' wi' nail,
    Clawks t'flesh off a brother's poar boans.

. " Theer's t'fathur heart-brocken wi' t'world an' its strife,
    That, turnin' away fro' his childer an' t'wife,
Lewks madly abaht for a roap or a knife
    To end an existence so cursed.
Theer's t'muther, 'at dladly wod dee if shoo mud,
For vainly shoo's lewkt tuv her brethren for food,
Bud shoo feels, thaw her babby is saukin' her blood,
    'At shoo cannot, an' munnot, dee t'first."

As t'angil tuke wing ah said " Fynd, if ya can,
A curly-wigged, puddin'-cheekt, double-chinn'd man,
He wor called by his friends an' his enemies ' Dan,'
    An' a shamrock he wears for a badge ;
He could squease aht o' t'Irish his thahsauds a-year—
An' if t'Pope an' his Cardinals hes him up theer,
Cut t'tail off a comet an' swing him dahn here,
    For O'Connell's a jewel to cadge."

Dan ventered on t'journey althau rayther risky,
Ah varry sooin felt a strong flavour o' whisky,
An' t'pen i' my fingers grew suddenly frisky,
    As he wrote tuv his brethren i' Yorks :—
"Bad cess to ye braakan the resht of a saint!
Is it nothing to you this sad outcry of want?
Ye're thinkin', may be, that ye won't, an' ye can't,
    Lose the use o' your knives an' your forks.

"They are starvan beyant there, thrue sons of the sod,
Just as dear as yourselves to our priests an' ther God,
Whol blaggards like you that should lighten ther load,
    Why, ye're aytan an' drinkan the full o' ye.
Ye shames ov Ould Ireland, ye'll alther, ah'll bet,
Ye'll be handy, my boys, an' ye'll pay off this debt,
Or the sorra a spoonful o' trayele ye'll get
    Wid the brimstone ah'll casht o'er the whole o' ye."

Soa, English or Irish, ye'll dew what ye can
Tard gettin' theas warkfowk a maathful o' scran ;
Remember, when givin', 'at he's the trew man
    'At pinches to give tuv another.
Owd England ul be merry England indeed,
When love gets ta strong for boath country an' creed,
An' ivry poar man tuv a fellah i' need
    Behaves like a man an' a brother.

OWD MOXY.

OWD Moxy rowt hard for his morsil o' breead,
    An' ta keep up his courage he'd sing,
Thau Time wi' his scythe hed maun t'crop on his eead,
    An' then pufft it away wi' his wing.

Reyt slavish his labour an' little his wage,
    His path tuv his grave wor bud rough,
Poor livin' an' 'ardships, a deal moar nur age,
    Hed swealed dahn his cannal to t'snuff.

One cowd winter morn, as he crept aht o' bed,
    T'owd waller felt dizzy an' soar :—
" Come, frame us some breykfast, Owd Duckfooit,"
      he said,
    " An' ah'll finish yond fence up at t'moor ;

" Al tew like a brick wi' my hammer an' mawl,
    An' ah'll bring hoam my honey to t'hive,
An' ah'll pay t'bit o' rent an' wer shop-score an' all,
    An' ah'll dee aht o' debt if ah live."

Soa Peg made his pobs an' then futtered abaht,
    An' temm'd him his tea into t'can,
Then teed up some bacon an' breead in a claht,
    Fur dearly shoo liked her owd man.

Then Moxy set aht on his wearisome way,
  Wadin' bravely thru t'snaw broth i' t'dark ;
It's a pity when fellahs at's wakely au' grey
  Hes ta walk for a mile to ther wark.

Bud summat that mornin' made Moxy turn back,
  Thau he 'ardly knew what it could meean,
Soa cudlin' Owd Peggy he gave her a smack,
  An' then startud fur t'common ageean.

All t'day a wild hurrikin wuther'd thru t'glen,
  An' then rusht like a fiend up to t'heeath ;
An' as Peggy sat knittin' shoo sed tuv hersen
  " Aw dear ! he'll be starruv'd to t'deeath."

An' shoo felt all that day as shoo'd ne'er felt afoar,
  An' shoo dreeadud yit hungar'd for neet ;
When harknin' an' tremlin' shoo ceard abaht t'doar
  A mutterin' an' shufflin' o' feet.

Five minits at after, Owd Peg, on her knees,
  Wor kussin' a foreead like stoan ;
An' to t'men at stood by her wi' tears i' ther ees,
  Shoo sed, " Goa, lads, an' leave ma aloan."

When they streytened his body, all ready for t'kist,
  It wor seen at he'd thowt of his plan,
For t'shop-score an' t'rent wor safe lockt in his fist,
  Soa he deed aht o' debt, like a man.

POLL BLOSSOM.

POLL Blossom, bonny blue-eed Poll,
    So nimal, streyt, an' tall,
Ye'd think, to see her on her pins,
    Shoo'd nivver knaw a fall.

Her parents, when they com to t'tahn,
    Wor varry, varry poor;
'Twor said 'at t'mice i' t'hahse tuke off,
    An' ne'er com' back na moar.

Her mother helpt t'owd wives ta wesh,
    An' brew ther stroakes o' malt;
Her father, wi' a one-wheeled cart,
    Cried—"Weight for weight for salt."

A careful, scrapin' pair they wor,
    As e'er samm'd t'muck off t'road,
An' t'world agreed ta hoin um boath,
    As schooil-lads hoins a toad.

Says Susy, "Times is varry hard,
    An' 'tisn't mich tha arns,
Ah'll boil Peg's dishclaht wi' some carbs,
    An' mak' a mess for t'barns."

Peg's husband rowt at t'ironwarks,
    An' lots o' meyt shoo gat,
Her mucky dishclaht, Susy said,
    Wor worth it's weight i' fat.

Two suet dumplins tue shoo made,
    An' popt um into t'pan ;
Says shoo, " They're just the varry thing
    For me an' my owd man."

Soa t'deep owd lass at dinner-time,
    Cried, " Nah then, Poll an' Dick,
Whichivver swallahs t'moast o' t'thin
    Sal hev t'bigg'st share o' t'thick."

Then t'greedy beggars fell ta wark,
    An' gate so blawn wi' t'broth,
Whol t'seet o' t'dumplins turned um sick,
    Soa t'owd uns gate um both.

Wi' ways like thease they carried on
    Thru gooid report an' ill,
T'owd father hawked, t'owd mother charred,
    An' Polly went to t'mill.

Ther nabors thowt all t'brass they hed
    Wod 'ardly crush a lahse,
When lo! they bowt some beeldin' grahnd
    An' belt thersens a hahse.

This done, Miss Blossom all at once
    Bethowt her who shoo wor,
Went up five storeys iu a day,
    An' capt boath rich an' poor.

An' thaw shoo scarce knew hah to spell,
  Nur hah to write a scrawk,
Shoo donn'd like one o' t'better soart,
  An' tried to mock ther talk.

Says one, " This world gets near its end,
  We see some seets, by t'meg,
A milner wi' a parasol,
    A veil, an' velvet beg."

One day Bet Turpin met wi' Poll,
  An' call'd aht, " How d'ye do ? "
Poll raised her eebrees tuv her hair,
  An' said, " Pray who are you ? "

" Ah'm t'lass," said Bet, wi' een like fire,
  An' face a furnace red,
" 'At wesht all t'shift ta hed i' t'world,
  Whol ta laid nakt i' bed."

" Hay, whoo ! " cried aht a lad 'at ceard
  Whot Bet said in her tift,
" Hay, whoo ! tha laid stark nakt i' bed
  Whol Betty wesht thy shift ! "

Five-score o' barns, let loose fro' t'skooil,
  Wor laakiu all abaht :
They left ther whips an' tops an' taws,
  An' joined i' t'hal an' shaat.

Poor Polly, like a hunted hare,
  Prickt ears an' off shoo went,
An' off went five-score skrikin' imps
  Like yowlin' haunds on t'scent.

Ther tonts au' yells wi' rage au' shame
  So tenged an' maddened Poll,
Shoo struke at t'first wi' all her meet,
  An' mesht her parasol.

Bud t'second time shoo tuke to t'road,
  A little nail ur peg
Stuck aht o' t'wall 'at shoo'd to pass
  An' clickt her velvit beg.

Her sweetheart's letters thear wor stowed,
  An' things shoo greeatly stored,
So when shoo turned an' saw 'twor goan
  Shoo stude stock still an' roared.

Just then t'young lad shoo'd fell'd afoar,
  An' left o' t'plat awf deead,
Com up wi' sink muck in his hand
  An' flung it 'at her cead.

Then Poll went at him, tooith au' nail,
  An' scazed an' pesht him dahn,
Bud as he fell to t'grund he rave
  Her bran new muslin gahn.

Then two police com up an' said,
  "What's all this row abaht?"
For answer t'five-score barns or moar
  Set up another shaat:—

"That's her 'at laid stark nakt i' bed
  Whol Betty wesht her shift."
T'owd cry hed 'ardly weel beguu
  When Poll thowt fit to skift.

Away shoo went, an' as shoo flew
   Her veil went up behynd,
An' lappin' rahnd a barber's powl
   Wor left to flap i' t'wind.

When t'lass 'ad spent her strength an' breath
   Shoo turned her head abaht,
An' slippin' off o' t'cawsa edge
   Shoo put her enkle aht.

Lost, loppard, bleedin', regg'd, an' worn,
   T'fine lady laid i' t'dyke,
Wi' two policemen shaatin' aht
   "Ger up, ye druckan tyke."

Bud Poll laid still, so one o' t'two
   Caar'd dahn an' raised her eead,
Then lewkin t'other streyt i' t'faas,
   He said, "Igow, shoo's deead."

Then t'other caar'd him dahn, an' said,
   "Yes, yes, she don't respire;"
Bud Poll tuke that a bat o' t'chops,
   An' said, "Shut up, ya liar!"

Wi' that boath t'bluecoits seazed her arms,
   An' rave her aht o' t'muck;
"Ah wish," said one, "'at we could get
   A seck cart or a truck."

A joiner in a shop aboon,
   Just near eniff to hear,
Called aht to t'two poleece, an' said,
   "Theer's my hand-barra theer."

When all wor square they samm'd up Poll,
    An' planted her on t'barra;
" We'll tak' up t'middle road," they said,
    " For t'cawsa's ovver narra."

" Wha, nah, tha lukes just like thysen ! "
    Cried aht a key-legg'd man,
" It's nobbud t'best o' t'better soart
    'At uses a sedan."

" For t'love o' mercy tak' ma hoam,"
    Said Poll to t'two poleece;
" If ye'll go faster ye sal hev
    A gooid awf-crahn a-piece."

" Here, mak' a whiplesh o' thy veil,"
    Said t'same young chap to Poll,
" An' prod thy two-legg'd cattle on
    Wi' t'heft o' t'parasol."

At last they reytcht her fathur's hahse—
    Her fathur oppen'd t'doar—
When ivvry woman, man, an' barn
    Set up a hay-bay moar.

" Aw Poll," they cried, " when next tha rides
    I' sitch a way as this,
If tha neglects to let us knaw
    Wese tak' it much amiss."

Beloved brethren, ye may learn,
    Fro' this poor girl's distress,
The sad effects o' worldly pride
    An' vanity i' dress.

NANNIE'S SOLILOQUY.

WELL, t'day's getten ovver ageean ;
　　Days wor nivver so long an' so dree !
Ah cannot tell what it can meean,
　　Nur what can be t'matter wi' me.
Ah ne'er felt so loanly afoar,
　　All t'world seems fair browt tuv a stand ;
So on Sunday ah oppen'd t'clock doar,
　　An' ah pusht forrad t'time wi' my hand.

He's lived wi' us nah for a year,
　　That queerist an' dumbist o' men,
Bud he's goan, an' ah cannot tell wheer,
　　An' he'll come ageean—noab'dy knaws when.
Ah wonder what moved him at dawn
　　To spring up an' leet ma my fire,
He'd plenty o' work of his awn,
　　An' moar nur eniff for his hire.

Then to think on't it's sich an a thing,
　　That yon cahs ivv'ry eemin' wor browt
Fro' t'Woodfield an' t'Holm an' t'Far Ing,
　　An' ah'd nivver once gien it a throwt.
Yond footman's some fea'ful nice hair,
　　He's clean an' lewks spicy to t'ee,
A chap to show off wi' at t'fair,
　　Bud he'd nean hae doin that mich for me.

When ah set off to t'party at t'Hall,
    Ah turned as ah nipt off at t'neuk ;
Poor Bill ! he wor leyned ageean t'wall,
    An' he lewkt sich a yonderly lewk.
Lots o' trinkets that footman hes gien,
    An' poor Bill could ware nowt on a lass,
Bud ah see nah thru t'tears o' my een
    'At his kindness wor better nur brass.

Ah sal murder that footman enah !
    He's getten on rayther ta fast ;
Good laws ! if he'd milked me a cah
    Theer's no knawin' what he'd hae assd.
Well, he's goan, an' my heart's sad an' soar,
    Bud ah'll up an' ah'll frame o' some wark,
An' ah'll think o' that fellah no moar—
    Now, nauther i' t'dayleet nur t'dark.

Still ah think it ud 'ardly be reyt
    To banish clean aht o' my mind
A lad that, be day or be neet,
    Wor awlus so humble an' kind.
A chap ah could ne'er understand,
    All deeds, bud no tattle nur fuss,
When he left he ne'er tuke ma by t'haud,
    Nor offered to gie ma a kuss ;

Bud afoar he gat reyt aht o' t'seet
    He lifted his sleeve tuv his ee,
An' ah'd give a year's wages to-neet
    To be suar he wor thinkin' o' me.
Heigh up ! an' heigh ho ! an' aw dear !
    My noddle's just reavy to crack !
Ah've wished, lad, tha'd nivver com'd here,
    Yit ah'm flayed 'at tha'll nivver come back.

BILL'S ANSWER.

SOA tha's wished 'at ah'd nivver com'd here,
    Yit tha'rt flayed ah sal nivver come back;
Hay! Nan, lass, this awf haar ur near
    Ah've been planted a-back o' this stack.

Yis, he com up as leet as a burd,
    That queerist an' dumbist o' men,
An' what's better, he's ceard ivv'ry word
    O' that talk 'at tha's hed wi' thysen!

Dunnot lowp like a hare off o' t'flooar,
    Nur frame to mak' off in a fuss,
Tak' warnin'—ah's tell tha no moar—
    If ta fidges ah'll gie tha a kuss.

Ah've summat to say, au' ah'll say't,
    Let tha fitter an' fling as ta will,
An' it happen ul pay tha to wait
    Just to hear a poor fellah like Bill.

Ah've covered ten mile wi' my hoof,
    Just to see tha an' speyk to tha here,
An' ah hoap that al stand as a proof
    'At ah doant come to scoff or to fleer.

Ah'm nut bahn to offer tha, Nan,
　A ribbin, a brooch, or a net,
Bud the heart of a true-hearted man—
　Wah, it's thine aht an' aht if tha'll hae't.

Witta come, lass, an' sweeten my cup,
　Witta say we mun nivver moar pairt,
An' as long as a bite an' a sup
　Can be won wi' 'ard workin' we'll share't?

An' to t'end o' this wearisome strife,
　I' t'front on tha awlus ah'll be,
To receive i' this battle o' life
　The blaws 'ats intended for thee.

Tha's seen, lass, hah hardly ah've rowt,
　An' tha's said ah'd no friends an' no brass,
Yit tha liked ma noa less when tha thowt
　'At poor Will could spend nowt on his lass.

Bud a thing 'at ah've nivver made knawn,
　To thee, Nan, ah'm bahn to declare :
My father's a farm ov his awn,
　An' Bill's boath his son an' his heir.

God bless my young burd in her nest,
　Shoo's dumb, for shoo's quite ovverfaced,
Soa shoo berries her eead i' my breast,
　An' shoo tightens her clasp o' my waist.

Well, a hoamstead is all varry weel,
　Bud we rate it at moar nur it's worth ;
Aw Nan, lass, this minnit ah feel
　It's love 'ats wer riches on earth.

T'WEYVER'S DEEATH.

AW, Mary, my heart's dlad an' fain
   Once moar to see t'shine o' thy ee,
I' darkness an' weakness an' pain
   Ah've watched an' ah've waited for thee.
Shoo'll suarly be comin', ah said,
   If it be but to bowster my cead,
It wor nobbud for this 'at ah stayed
   Soa long ameng t'deein' an' t'deead.

Ah've leng'd, whol ah 'ardly could bide,
   To tell tha what's passin' within,
Bud nah when ta't set by my side
   Ah cannot tell hah to begin.
Ah mud just as weel tell tha my case:
   Ah've a doctor, a nurse, an' all that,
Bud—don't let me breathe i' thy face—
   All ther skill an' ther care is ta lat.

Aw, Mary, as dear as my life
   Ah've loved tha this monny a year,
If ah ne'er tried to mak' tha my wife
   'Twor becos that ah felt tha so dear.
An' ah've thowt 'at tha's liked me as weel,
   An' that clasp o' thy hand mak's it knawn,
Soa—lat as it is, lass—ah feel
   That i' t'face o' two worlds tha'rt my awn.

E

Thau here ah wor nivver nowt worth,
   An's a pauper, as hard as ah've striven,
Yit as suar as ah've loved tha on earth
   So suar ah sal love tha i' heaven.
Dus ta hear that queer saand i' my chest?
   It's a sign 'at life's clock's bahn to stand ;
Let's leyn my poor eead on thy breast,
   An' dunnot leave off o' my hand.

I s'd a liked tha ta sing ma that hymn,
   That sweet hymn tha sung ma t'last May ;
Bud my seet's growin' claady an' dim,
   An' all things is fadin' away.
Yit still ah can see thy dear face,
   As it sinks like a sun aht o' t'seet ;
Bud a glory is fillin' this place,
   So that t'shaddahs lewks rosy an' breet.

To see what ah see tha'd be charmed—
   The fields wheer i' childhood we trod ;
An' my sowl is all leetud an' warmed
   With the love an' the presence of God.
All's peaceful an' fresh as the morn,
   All faces seems fain 'at ah've come,
An' softly an' sweetly aboon
   Some angel plays " Home, home, sweet home."

Ah dreamed that sore sorras ah'd knawn,
   That my lot wor ta hunger an' weep,
Bud ah see nah, by t'leet o' this dawn,
   That my life's been a feverish sleep.
Ah'm near it—that bewtiful land,
   Wheer sweeat drops an' tears nivver fall,
Wheer brother tak's brother by t'hand,
   An' the Lord like a sun shines on all.

THE OLD MAN'S LAST SOLILOQUY.

FOR me throughout th' unchanging year
    The sky is dark, the sun is cold,
All things seem always dead and sere,
    For Spring-time comes not to the old ;
Wife, sister, daughter—none is near,
    But strangers crowd my haunts, and say,
"Thou hast no work, no portion here,
    Thy world is passed away."

All things are cold and dumb—the grove
    Is silent, hushed the winds and streams,
And voices, all whose tones were love,
    Are echoes only heard in dreams.
Shadows, alas ! are all I own ;
    But airy shapes around me come,
And dear ones gather, one by one,
    Within my ruined home.

Old scenes, old faces dear and kind,
    Have left me in the dark alone ;
Love, friendship, labour, lie behind ;
    Before, the near but dim unknown.
This world, so dark and cold alway,
    Fast disappears in utter night,
But thro' its darkness comes a ray
    Of strange unearthly light.

Lo! faintly, and as yet afar,
　　Dim shapes and flitting glories swim,
And in the solemn hush I hear
　　The song of star-crowned cherubim;
Nearer and nearer still they come,
　　While beams, shot down by Mercy, show
The children that made glad my home—
　　They call me, and I go.

THE SISTER OF MERCY.

THE voice that can so sweetly sing
    Hath counsels for the evil hour,
Blest words! that to the spirit bring
    Health, wisdom, fortitude, and power;
Her heart's pure love, come woe or weal,
    Were more than all the world is worth,
A balm that well might soothe or heal
    All sorrow known on earth.

She near the sick bed oft is seen,
    Her hands the fatherless have clad;
Yet the world marvels at her mien—
    Unwed, yet hopeful; lone, yet glad.
Poor homeless dying slaves of lust
    She sought and healed, and kept them whole,
Till from the loathed polluted dust
    Upsprang the stainless soul.

Plain is her garb, and coarse her fare,
    Yet humbled wealth in vain hath wooed;
Even genius may not hope to share
    That maiden's holy solitude.
And know ye why the good and brave
    So vainly sought their worth to prove?
There is an unforgotten grave,
    Where lies her buried love.

Oft in the still and happy night
　　He comes—the pure, the glorified—
He comes with heavenly love and light
　　To cheer his unforgotten bride.
Bright grows the hope, and strong the faith,
　　The faith that sees the world to come,
Her spirit leaps the gulf of death
　　And feels the peace of home.

The low, sweet voice is heard again,
　　Her head is on his bosom laid,
His lips but touch her brow, and then
　　She wakens—weeping, comforted.
Not vainly, then, the night and day
　　To holy cares and toils are given,
Since labours, poor and mean as they,
　　Brought down that smile from heaven.

NIGHT VISIONS.

SWEET are the long hours of the solemn night,
　That bring the peace that hovers o'er the dead,
For scenes, illumined by no earthly light,
　Rise in the chaos round the pillowed head;
The Eden world my sinless childhood knew
Springs from the grave of time to bless my view.

The soft warm wind is scented with the breath
　Of flowers that perished in my babyhood,
The melody of voices hushed in death
　Re-echoes merrily thro' vale and wood;
My home, my first home, seen thro' gushing tears,
Shines in the sun of long-departed years.

Beside our cottage stands the ancient oak,
　O'er which we mourned as for a father slain,
And all uninjured by the woodman's stroke
　Spreads its paternal arms and lives again;
And there beneath its boughs sits many a form
Long since consigned to darkness and the worm.

But where is she, the glory of my youth,
　Whose absence made the crowd a solitude?
Life had no ills when she was near to soothe—
　The innocent! the beautiful! the good!
Oh, joy, joy, joy! she comes once more to bless;
Let silence, poor dumb harp, my bliss express.

Cherubic lore with haloes girds her brow,
    But all the seraph fills her pitying eyes,
And warnings, given in whispers sweet and low,
    Fall on my ears like music from the skies;
Her tears I see, her trembling hand I feel—
Angel of light! I know thou lov'st me still.

'Tis gone! but ere the vision passed away
    Her finger pointed to her home above;
And looks, than words more melting, seemed to say
    That sin alone can sever those who love,
And that our hearts but tasted here below
The heaven that goodness may for ever know.

Old home, old scenes, I seek—I haunt ye yet,
    Tho' there sad changes me and mine befell,
Tho' strangers there in me a stranger meet,
    There is no place on earth I love so well.
Forget not, oh my soul, in dreams of pride
Or vain pursuits, who there have lived and died.

HUMAN PROGRESS.

TO man, the naked, impotent, were given
    Courage and skill—the two best gifts of heaven;
With bolder front he then began to roam,
Dislodged the wild beast, and possessed his home.
Struck by his club, the gnashing panther died,
And clothed the victor with his princely hide;
The lion, growling o'er his fleecy prey,
Awed by his burning eye-ball, slunk away;
Caught in his flying noose, the affrighted horse
Resigned to him his swiftness and his force.
At length the furnace roared and raged and glowed,
Till from its fires the spade and ploughshare flowed
Then melancholy wastes, by labour tilled,
Put forth the rose and, robed in beauty, smiled.

On the sea shore his straining eyes surveyed
Far distant lands in brighter hues arrayed,
He dares the dangerous and the doubtful path,
Launches the bark, and mocks the ocean's wrath.
Nursed for the battle—born to be supreme—
He wars with all things—all things war with him.

At last the sage, with holy triumph fraught,
Grasps in his hand imperishable thought;

Eternal voices whispered from the grave,
And age to age its treasured wisdom gave.
Victorious man, with unabated breath,
Lives thro' all time to scoff at baffled Death.

Fraught with the wisdom of unnumbered years,
See what a halo round his brow appears ;
On proud dominion's airy height he stands,
Holding the reins of nature in his hands.
He bids the breezes toil, the ocean waves
His burdens bear like meek and conquered slaves ;
Sublime inventions teach his soul to slight
The eagle's swiftness and the lion's might.

Woes, wants, and ills, since earth's primeval hour,
Have but matured intelligence and power ;
Man from each bitter wrings some priceless sweet—
From suffering, patience, wisdom from defeat,
From wants ingenious thought, from effort force,
Greatness from sorrow, glory from the curse.

Each flower of joy, that time and being cheers,
Was won from thorns, and nursed with sweat and tears ;
Laws, arts, religion—all things great or good
Were born in anguish and baptised in blood.
Strengthened with strife, and dignified with woes,
Man to the stature of the angel grows.

T'SPICY MAN.

A TWO month sin' ur moar, thear coom
   To lodge wi' Widda Blan
A fella, known to t'lads abaht
   By t'name o' t'Spicy Man.

A grander, spiffer-lewkin' chap
   'Twor ne'er yur luck to meet;
He lewkt just like a gentleman
   'At awned boath sides o' t'street.

A white hat trimmed wi' crape he ware,
   An' velvet-collared coit,
An' walked, bigow, as stiff an' streyt
   As if he'd swallud t'poyt.

His hair hung dahn like rattan tails
   Below his shiny hat,
An' spraatud aht fro' t'ovver lip
   I' t'manner of a cat.

Gowld rings an' studs an' walkin' cane,
   An' watchguard crossin' t'breast,
Set off this furst o' gentlemen
   I' t'first o' t'feshun drest.

T'owd wives come aht o' t'hahse to gloar
　　At t'man an' t'duds an' t'stick,
An' childer threng i' mischief cut
　　As if they'd spied owd Nick.

Poor beggars mungin' cowd pottate,
　　Ur singin' sengs i' t'street,
Nipt inta ginnels, and wor dumb
　　Whol he gate aht o' t'seet.

Young lasses tluthered rahnd him oft
　　To hear his sawvy blab,
An' cabmen touched ther greasy hats
　　An' cried aht, " Cab, sir, cab ? "

Bud whot he wor, or whot he did,
　　Capt t'moast o' t'fowks abaht ;
T''schooilmaister tried by t'rewl o' three,
　　Bud couldn't mak' it aht.

They axt t'owd sowger what he thowt ;
　　T''owd sowger gav' a groan,
An' said at thame 'at kept a shop
　　Wod freat when he wor goan.

Bet Backbite called him t'markit quack,
　　An' said 'at onny day
Shoo'd bet a crahn he'd popt an' drunk
　　His tapeworms an' his tray.

T''owd Quakeriss i' t'koil skep hat,
　　'At lived i' Dobson Coart
An' sell'd ut moofins, set him dahn
　　For one o' t'better soart.

Some said 'at he'd a nunk i' t'East,
   A dried-up wizzand tyke,
'At wiped his noas o' five-pund noates
   Then flung um into t'dyke.

Then theer wor gurt istaats i' t'Sahth
   Belongin' t'Heir at Law,
An' he wor t'chap if reyt wor doin,
   An' that he'd let um knaw.

He nobbud wantid twenty pahnd
   To put i' t'lawyer's hand,
An' then he tlaimed the hoal consarn—
   Coil, timber, hahse an' land.

Sal Kitchin popt her tlock an' drawers,
   An' sell'd up knife an' fork,
To put him on whol t'uncle deed,
   Or t'case come on at York.

Soa t'Spicy Man did varry weel
   For near hand awf a year,
He milked the simple, laid i' bed,
   An' laughed fro' ear to ear.

At times he'd paddle up an' dahn
   Wi' papers in his paw,
Letters fro' t'Indies sealed wi' black,
   Or parchment deeds o' law.

But t'peacock stript o' feathers lewks
   No better nur a toad,
An' theer's an end to t'breetist day,
   A turn i' t'longist road.

One frosty morn, at ten o'clock,
 A simple-lewkin' man
Popt in, as if be accident,
 To lewk at Widda Blan.

    •

This eeasy, oppen-hearted chap
 Sat dahn i' t'chair by t'hob,
An' axed her if her better rahms
 Worn't rented by a nob.

A deeal o' questions follad t'furst,
 An' all 'at t'widda said
He wrate it in a red-backed book,
 Whol t'lodger laid i' bed.

At last he added all on't up,
 As if't hed been a sum,
Clapt his forfingur tuv his noas,
 An' tell'd her to be mum.

That varry day, at twelve o'clock,
 A lady, donn'd i' black,
Nipt slyly into Widda Blan's
 An' assd for " Bahncin' Jack."

Bud t'widda said 'at noa such chap
 'At shoo knew on wor theer,
For t'oanly man shoo hed wor called
 Augustus Edward Vere.

" Go tell him," said t'owd dame i' black,
 " I want an interview;
" I've seen his notice for a wife,
 " An' think that ah shall do."

" Be quick an' tell him, what, no doubt,
   He'll be right glad to hear,
That I've an income from the funds
   Of eighty pounds a year."

The minit that ahr Spicy Man
   Hed ceard Dame Blan's report,
He whewd his bedcloas into t'air
   An' bahnced aht in his shurt.

Shaved, wesht an' brusht, an' oiled, wi' smiles
   'At rake fro' ear to ear,
He entered t'rahm an' made his bow
   To t'eighty pahnd i' t'year.

"Oh, no!" he cried, "it cannot be—
   An' yet upon my life—
Oh, heaven! that I should see this hour—
   It is—it is my wife!"

" Yes, monster! villain! traitor! brewt!
   Thy wretched wife I am ;
Com hoam an' see hah nice it is
   To watch yond childer clam."

What moar shoo said wor nivver knawn,
   For t'widda ceard na moar,
Bud startin' up, wi' t'news shoo'd ceard
   Shoo flew fro' doar to doar.

At last, wi' quite a sweggrin' air,
   He com aht into t'street ;
Bud owls an' sich like birds o' prey
   Lewks noan sa weel i' t'leet.

An' when ya pearkt him clois at hand
　　He fell away, by t'meg,
Like a grand sceue at t'theatre,
　　To slapdash an' a reg.

He seemed a bunch o' seemin's—all
　　Veneer an' paint an' sham,
Fuff, fuzball, mooinshine, coffin lid,
　　A walkin' Brummagam.

Just then some chaps, 'at wanted brass
　　'At they could nivver get,
Com up, an' sware 'at he sud leave
　　Ahr taanship aht o' debt.

Soa reyt at t'Spicy Man they went,
　　An' brayed him black an' blew;
Then t'women tluthered rahnd, an' rave
　　His coit up t'back i' two.

Bud t'warst i' t'lot wor Sossidge Bet,
　　A fea'ful fierce owd witch,
'At kept a stall by t'public hahse
　　An' sell'd pig fit an' sich.

My stars! shoo yell'd aht, " Ho'd 'im, lads,
　　An' let 'im feel my gripe;
He owes ma ivv'ry awpne piece
　　For twenty pund o' tripe."

Ta crahn it, t'mob rave up his coit
　　Ta ribbins an' ta regs,
Then teed um on ta besom steyls
　　An' hoistud um for flegs.

" Paleeee ! paleeee !" he shaated aht,
    When up com two ur three—
" It's weel," they said, "tha wants us, lad,
    For long we've wantud thee.

" An' nah we'se tak' tha dahn to t'hoil,
    For we can due na less,
Cos t'wife au' t'childer, does ta see,
    Hes lived for months o' t'cess."

Wi' that t'paleeecmen waved ther sticks,
    An' tried ta tlear ther way,
Whol t'crahd behint went two by two,
    All shaatin aht, " Hurrah !"

An' just to work his feelin's up
    To t'height o' shame au' rage,
T'owd Fahndry Band com aht an' played
    The " Rogue's March" dahn to t'cage.

An' soa wi' t'rummist carryin's on
    'At e'er wor seen ur eeard,
The Spicy Man fro' t'face o' t'earth
    At that time disappeared.

THE SWANS.

*Written after seeing for the first time the beautiful pair in
Peel Park, the gift of L. C. Hill, Esq.*

WELCOME, ye queens of lake and pool !
How meet it is that ye should come
Where art and nature make a home
For creatures rare or beautiful.

There is no castle old and hoar,
No meer, isle-dotted, fringed with woods,
No shady, windless solitudes,
That keep the Sabbath evermore.

Yet scorn ye not the mill and mart,
Birds of proud mien and high estate ;
The city's grimy democrat
Shall greet ye with a loyal heart.

Beauty is art's eternal theme ;
And worthy are ye of a place
Among the varied shapes that grace
The bard or painter's glorious dream.

So live and reign, ye royal pair,
For here a strong and jealous guard
Shall bid the pavement spare the sward,
And trees, not chimneys, scent the air.

And often here an outcast race,
    Escaped the chain and prison latch,
    Shall walk these green retreats, and catch
Brief glimpses of our Father's face.

LIGHTS AND SHADOWS.

HUSHED is the din of grating wheels,
  No sounds the sleeping city start,
  O'er silent street and empty mart
The Sabbath's holy quiet steals.

Heaven sends to earth its own deep peace—
  An angel of the Lord appears
  Within this vale of sweat and tears,
Whose whisper bids the tempest cease.

White cloudlets, by the breeze upborne,
  Sail gently thro' the stainless blue,
  While song-birds, glistening yet with dew,
Pour out their welcome to the morn.

The sunshine, like the smile of God,
  Bids all the tribes of earth rejoice,
  While the lark's anthem, like the voice
Of joy, goes upwards from the sod.

Yet here, where soft winds o'er me sweep,
  Where faint and far-off melodies
  Blend with the slumb'rous hum of bees
To soothe heart sorrow, I must weep.

Once more, once more o'er field and sky,
  Look forth, my sister, and be glad;
  Oh! let no hour of thine be sad—
So fair, so early doomed to die.

As blows the summer's fragrant breath
  On tinted cheek and marble brow,
  Thou smilest, for thou feel'st not now
The shadow of the wings of death.

Yet the frail flowers, that round thee wave,
  Will long outlive thee; and the bird,
  Whose song even now in heaven is heard,
Will sing its anthem o'er thy grave.

So, while the world looks young and green,
  While hill and woodland, field and grove,
  Ring with the sounds of joyous love,
I go where I may weep unseen.

THE TRADESMAN'S DREAM.

POOR wasted bondsman—desk and mart
   Claimed all his hours, and everywhere
   A haunting, ever-present care
Hung like a night-mare o'er his heart.

For him there came no terms of mirth,
   Like showers on deserts; ne'er did he
   Fill his own heart with childish glee
When children gambolled on his hearth.

To him, alas, was all unknown
   The bounding joy the beast can feel,
   When, stript of chains, his lifted heel
Glints in the slow-descending sun.

He died; and even the good and just
   Said that his soul's intense desire
   For gain had, like a hidden fire,
Changed him to ashes and to dust.

And yet he was not what he seemed,
   For when at last o'er the still frame
   A brief and happy slumber came,
Like night on brawling streets, he dreamed :

Far from his old unlovely haunts
　　He built his peaceful future home,
　　And bade the stream and sunshine come
To nurse his darlings—flowers and plants.

Oft in a green and sunny spot,
　　Where swung the little song-bird's nest,
　　He sate and took his thoughtful rest—
Past care, past heart-ache all forgot.

And oft, by deeper musings awed,
　　He sought the depths of summer woods,
　　And in their pillared solitudes
Remembered his forgotten God.

And kindly, loving deeds were done,
　　That made the poor man call him friend ;
　　So, calmly to their solemn end,
The days passed o'er him, one by one.

A DIRGE.

Sung o'er the graves in the Crimea.

FAR o'er the deep the weary moon sinks down,
    And night winds utter sounds of woe and pain,
Sad as the voice that once on Gilboa's crown
    Mourned o'er the mighty in the battle slain.

Paled, as with tears, our melancholy star
    Looks o'er the desert, cold and white and dim ;
While, low and drear, the ocean from afar
    Sings thro' the solemn night your funeral hymn.

Proudly, brave youths, a warrior's meed to earn,
    With trump and banner went ye to the wars,
And joyously ye sang, " We will return
    With trophies and with honourable scars.

" Or if we die, the thunder of our guns,
    The wild, mad onrush to a soldier's grave,
Old England's ' Well done ' o'er her fallen sons—
    These will make soft the death-beds of the brave."

Not such your doom, tho' such the fate ye chose,
    True hearts and brave, a nation's strength and boast,
With tears of shame your country names your foes—
    Famine and toil, and nakedness and frost.

My brave, forsaken brothers, who can tell
   How slow your days, how drear your nights of woe,
Ere hope and strength departed, and ye fell
   To sleep and stiffen on the Crimean snow?

Dread shade of Cromwell, didst thou hear their groans,
   And know'st thou that thy country needs thy sword
To smite vain fools that dare to sit on thrones,
   And wave far off th' anointed of the Lord?

THE DAISY.

FLOWERS bloom and fade, suns rise and set,
　　And all things hasten to their fall ;
　But ere the last sad change of all,
Once more, dear flow'ret, have we met.

Once more beside that dear old home,
　　As in that earliest, sunniest time,
　　When all things revelled in their prime,
And the wide earth contained no tomb.

As in those days when youth and health
　　Our lives as in a glory shrined,
And the poor field flowers were the wealth
　　Of " Ormus and of Ind."

Ah, happy season—blest abode
　　That, thro' the tears of fond regret
　　And mists of dark'ning days, even yet
Shines like the Paradise of God.

Earth's generations turn their eyes
　　Back to the infant days of time,
　　Ere sorrow, born of brooding crime,
Had severed mortals from the skies.

For us, our childhood, saith the sage,
  Is that bright dream that men recall,
The poets long-gone golden age—
  The Eden—lost to all.

Fate treads us down with iron hoof,
  And changes bring us pain and ill;
  But changes, darker, sadder still,
Now meet thy pure eyes' meek reproof.

For the soul tints the cheek with fire
  At sight of her diviner form,
  Bruised like a reed by passion's storm,
And fouled with sin's unholy mire.

While thou could'st feel the sun afar,
  And from the mire, the worm, the night,
Like the fallen sister of a star,
  Rise up into the light.

DESPAIR.

NOW, wife, let me out, I say,
    I will strive with my fate no more;
I have travell'd for scores of miles,
    I have halted from door to door.

Work ! work ! work ! give me work, I cried,
    No matter what sort it be,
So the meed be a slice of bread
    For the famishing babes and thee.

I have begged, I have sought in vain,
    I have done all that mortal can ;
So, wife, get thee out of the way
    Of a fearless and hopeless man.

A whisper has come from the pool
    That has told me how this may end,
And the knife and the rope have looked
    Like the face of a faithful friend.

But first the oppressor shall know
    That I value not limb or life,
If he buries his gold in his heart
    I will dig up the hoard with my knife.

A curse on the cruel rich,
  On the fat of the land o'erfed,
And a curse on all lords and laws
  That stand between me and bread.

And a curse on the God above,
  That sees, with a pitiless eye,
My babes, that never have sinned,
  Of cold and of hunger die.

THY KINGDOM COME.

THROUGH the long winter, drear and bare,
    The corpse-like earth lay stark and dumb,
Breathing the mute, unspoken prayer,
    " O Sun-God, let thy kingdom come.

" Dark, dark the nights, the days how slow ;
    The silent stream, the naked tree,
And dim wide wastes of ghostly snow—
    Father in heaven, these wait for thee."

Awake to life and all its joys,
    Come forth, thou shrouded sleeper, come,
'Tis thus, oh earth, thy master's voice
    Calls thee, dead lazar, from thy tomb.

The snows like phantoms disappear,
    The ice snaps like a captive's chain,
Glad music hails the op'ning year,
    And the world's saviour shines again.

But generations come and go,
    And the slow ages rise and set ;
Ah me ! how sad it is to know
    That the soul's springtime comes not yet.

Dark, dark the night around, above,
   And hard and dead the spirit Earth ;
Oh Thou, whose beams are truth and love,
   Sun of the unseen heavens, shine forth !

Our hearts grow heavy day by day,
   Shiv'ring with cold, and lost in gloom,
With foreheads in the dust we pray,
   " Thy kingdom come ! Thy kingdom come ! "

NAPOLEON.

HOW oft our world has felt the ire
    Of earthquake, whirlwind, flood, and fire.
How oft on nature's quiet all
The rebel elements of earth
Have burst their bonds, and bounded forth,
As if to work creation's fall,
And whirl the glorious forms we see
In ruins through infinity.
Yet earth endures, and fresh and green
And lovely in th' eternal sun
Smiles as when first from darkness won,
While scarce a trace or stain is seen
To show that these have ever been.

The earthquake's hidden fire is quenched,
The ocean wave has sunk to sleep,
The whirlwind—whose wild onrush wrenched
The cedar from the mountain steep,
And blended in the darken'd air
Homes, harvests, all things dear and fair—
At last, amid some lone wood, heaves
A faint, low, melancholy sigh,
As if beneath the forest leaves
It sought a place in which to die.

Proud spirit! thus shall't be with thee,
Even such the end thy pride shall see;
Monarchs, in thy extinguished eye,
Now see not writ their destiny.
No more thy tongue, from thrones of state,
Speaks as its own the words of fate;
Thy sword is sheathed, thy thunder dumb,
A calm o'er all the world has come,
And mortals have beheld in thee
The last great plague our race shall see;
Thy sword is sheathed, thy banner furled,
And never more beneath the sky
Shall man in madness deify
The desolators of the world.

Millions of men no more shall stand
Soulless, that one imperial soul,
As his own limbs, may move the whole;
Millions no more, with steel and brand,
Mar earth with ashes, blood, and tears,
Perish like wrecks on the broad sea,
Or writhe on land, that one may be
The god of fools in after years.

The prophet-muse shall speak thy doom,
The sentence of the age to come:
Thy lurid halo shall depart,
Thy glory be thy curse and shame;
For time shall show thee as thou art—
All monstrous, and thy mighty name,
That, uttered in all nations, came
Like thunder on the ears of men,
While the pale cheek sent back again
The blood upon the frighted heart;

G

Even that shall perish on the tide
Of time.   A little longer ride
Majestic, sombre, and alone;
Then, like a wreck'd and broken ship,
Go down into the tongueless deep,
No more for ever to be known.

THE IRISH GIRL.

OUTWORN with travel, toil, and heat,
    Yon quiet spot she may not pass,
But rests her bare and blistered feet
    Upon the soft green grass.

The basket, stored with tiny ware,
    The burden on her weary back,
The beads and crucifix declare
    The Colleen Erinach.

A cloud is on her darkened brow,
    Tho' beautiful she is and young;
Wit, laughter, music, stir not now
    Her wild and ringing tongue.

A piper, blind, and old, and grey,
    Sate down with reapers at their ale
She stopped, she list'ned to the lay—
    A love-song of the Gael.

The piper played right merrily,
    Right merrily the chorus rang;
Ochone! it was the lullaby
    Her buried mother sang.

But this is not the mountain glen
　That echoed once the joyous lay;
The friends that raised the chorus then,
　Alas! how far away.

Back, like a bird o'er land and wave,
　Her wailing, rushing spirit passed,
And o'er a far-off lowly grave
　Fell faint and sick at last.

Few, few the words, and low and drear,
　In which that voice of sorrow spake—
Och! mother dear, och! mother dear,
　My heart, my heart will break.

And think not, proud and high-born one,
　That outcast's woe than thine is less;
Poor, banish'd children, ye alone
　That orphan's grief may guess.

Oh, soothe that virgin's sore distress,
　Queen virgin, piteous, undefiled;
Stoop, crownèd mother, stoop and bless
　That world-forsaken child.

OLD SCENES.

ON the fair home of young delight,
   On scenes of early life and love,
The morning sunbeams, warm and bright,
   Fall, like a glory, from above.

Far down the gently-sloping hill
   Lie chapel, cottage, farm, and fold,
The shining dam, the ruined mill,
   The brookside pathway dear of old.

Old melodies—I hear them all,
   The wind's faint whispers, fitful, weird,
The cornmill's far-off waterfall,
   The wild bee, and the song of bird.

But where are now the form and face
   That once my dreamy rambles shared ?
Where now the landscape's breathing grace,
   Blue-eyed, rose-tinted, golden-haired ?

The cup that held life's precious wine
   Was shivered ere its brim was kissed,
Weeping, I saw the draught divine
   Exhaling in untasted mist.

Yet, scoff I not at noble aims,
  Nor, with sour heart and nostril curled,
Say love and friendship are but names,
  And a base hunger rules the world.

Grief long ago has lost its power,
  For now I know it cannot be
That time should wither in an hour
  The hopes that grasped eternity.

The first pure flowers of human love,
  The silent bliss, the perfect trust,
These, blighted here, shall bloom above
  And grace the Eden of the just.

So hope yet blossoms thro' the years,
  And those dear spots her feet have trod
Still, thro' the mists of happy tears,
  Shine like the paradise of God,

Tho' wasted now my joyous prime,
  My days are cloudless and serene,
The memories of that olden time
  Keep heart and soul still young and green.

Far from me let base hopes be hurled;
  Let low ambitions ne'er be thine;
What profit if I gain the world,
  And stain the soul once linked to thine?

Like a small streamlet of the waste
  That, running, wets the mountain grass,
So may I, as to thee I haste,
  Make life look greener as I pass.

And should I lose, in moods unblest,
　My faith in goodness, love, and truth,
Blue-eyed, rose-tinted, golden-tressed,
　Return, oh vision of my youth.

THE CAPTIVITY.

SEE high in air the banners float,
  And hark the trumpets herald note,
The martial tramp, and din ;
Haste ! for the mighty may not wait ;
Ope, Babylon, thy widest gate,
And let thy monarch in.

He comes ! he comes ! the warrior king !
And shouts thro' all the city ring
That shake her marble palaces.
With pride, with joy the victor sees
Ten thousand shields around him blaze,
And, as they flash a triple day,
On all that long and vast array,
His eyes grow brighter as they gaze.

As thy tall ships, oh Tyrus, rise
Above the burdened ocean waves,
That bear, like tamed and tutored slaves,
To the world's ends thy merchandise ;
So towers the scourge of Judah high
O'er all that flaming pageantry,
And mad with power, and drunk with blood,
Moves with the heaving human flood.

But when around the victor's car
Appear the sacred spoils of war,
Telling how rapine and the sword
Have stained thy holy temple, Lord,
Then all at once the trumpets bear
Their loudest welcome to his car ;
Then minstrels to the joyous air
Fling music from a thousand strings,
While to the distance, faint and dim,
Rolls the deep anthem lauding him
Whose footstool is the neck of kings.

Lo, guarded by the lifted spear,
The captives follow in the rear.
Slowly they come, for they are faint
With heat and travel, thirst and want ;
Sadly they come, for they have lost
What mortals love and cherish most ;
And mute they come, for cries and tears
Relieve not anguish such as theirs.
The visions of a sunny past—
Of homes, old haunts, and loved ones—rise
To mock their voiceless agonies.
So Eden's outcasts, when the blast
Rushed thro' the roaring wilderness,
Mourned in some cavern's dark recess
O'er moments spent in Paradise.

Mourn, captive daughter, scatter now
The dust upon thy crownless brow,
For song and dance in wooded vale
No virgin band at eventide meets.
Alas ! thy maidens now bewail
The youth that sleep in rusting mail

In Salem's solitary streets;
Thy matrons hear upon the wind
The cry of infants left behind;
Thy sacred fathers, old and grey,
Have fallen and perished by the way;
Thy priests, with faces earthward bowed,
As slaves shall stand before the crowd,
And chant, to make the heathen mirth,
The strain that Zion warbled forth.
Perchance, in Nebo's Temple sing
The psalms of Judah's poet-king,
And when the breaking, bursting heart
Bids from the tongue the strain depart,
A tyrant's taunt shall wound thy ears,
And laughter mock thy bitter tears.

HYMN FOR THE NEW YEAR.

WHY should we mourn as others mourn,
  Whose heritage is here?
Let songs of joy, from thankful hearts,
  Salute the new-born year.

Tho' brief the days, and drear the nights,
  The vapours chill and dun,
Behind them and above them all
  For ever shines the sun.

The plains whose sheaves shall feed the world
  Lie sealed in ice and snow,
So hearts as cold and dead as they
  Shall heavenly fruitage grow.

Let not the Winter's gloom and cold
  Bid Faith and Hope expire,
For day by day the blessed sun
  Mounts higher still and higher.

So from the soul that evil hates
  Shall doubt and darkness flee,
And day by day each day shall bring
  More light, O Lord, from Thee.

Then let us sing the night away,
  While tempests rage and howl,
For truth, like buried seed, shall live,
  And plenty fill the soul.

As warmth and sunshine yet shall stream
  O'er frozen hill and plain,
So light shall flood the inner world,
  And Love the conqueror reign,

HYPOCRISY.

THE owl crept out of the old oak tree,
    As the sun was sinking fast,
" Oh ! weary and long was the night," said he,
    " But the daylight comes at last.

" Yon orb that filled with a blinding haze
    The world with its fields and skies,
Like a coward shrinks from the steadfast gaze
    Of the morning's thousand eyes.

" What a life of sorrow and sad unrest
    Have the creatures that shun the light;
How the ploughman cursed his stumbling beast,
    As it toiled through the sultry night.

" For needful rest, or for solemn prayer,
    Should the hours of darkness be,
But the throstle and skylark filled the air
    With their godless revelry.

" Poor blinded things, whom a thousand lamps
    Cannot light to their insect prey,
Yet they sing as they shiver in twilight damps
    Of light and of heaven, ha ! ha !

" See the mice from their holes come forth to steal,
  Creeping softly across the plain,
Of the thieves 'tis just I should make a meal,
  For they eat up the farmer's grain.

" And I hear in the thorn the starving brood
  Of the linnets the kestrel slew,
I cannot endure their cries for food,
  So in pity I'll eat them too.

" Oh, Justice and Mercy I dearly love,
  In Wisdom and Truth I delight,
By day I enjoy the smile of Jove,
  And the sleep of the just by night."

Ah ! human owls in the world are rife,
  Who mistake the night for day,
Who join false faith to the evil life,
  Who devour the poor—and pray.

THE BETRAYED.

SADLY and silently roll down her tears,
   Sorrow in secret will ever be hers,
Cold is her chamber and lonesome and bare,
None who once loved her will visit her there.

Friendship and Love to that desolate home
Never have been, perhaps never may come;
Over thee, frail one, the tear has been shed,
Those who once owned thee now mourn thee as dead.

Near us, yet far off, an exile at home,
Neighbours and playmates are strangers and dumb,
Even when they see thee thy form like a ghost,
Doth but remind them of one that is lost.

Father and mother, and sister and kin,
All have forsaken the daughter of sin,
Quickly, poor outcast, go down to thy grave,
None will e'er seek thee to soothe or to save.

Darkness besets thee around and above,
Darkness that knows not one sunbeam of love,
Soon wilt thou enter a gloom where no ray
Falls on the pathway that leads back to day.

Father, stern father, fallen, fallen tho' she be,
Once, fair and sinless, she played on thy knee,
Sin-spots are thine, man, unwashed with thy tears,
Broader and darker than any of hers.

Mother, stern mother, wake up from thy rest,
Seek thou the lost one that hung from thy breast,
Frown not but know thou that love was her sin,
Love, ah! how nearly to virtue akin.

Sadly and silently roll down her tears,
Sorrow in solitude ever is hers,
Back to your bosoms restore her forgiven,
Else seek ye never a Father in Heaven.

THE BROTHERS.

OH ! the night is dreary,
    Cold my limbs and weary,
Brother, whither go we now ?
    Land and homes are near us,
    Warmth and wine would cheer us,
Wherefore should we further row ?

    " Brother, know that races
    Heaven-bound turn their faces
Quickly, sadly from that shore."
    There the wave-worn meeting,
    Smile on cup of greeting,
Sink to sleep and wake no more.

    See ! across the breakers
    Signal lights of wreckers
Lure us to the hidden rock.
    Undismayed, unswerving,
    Heart and sinew nerving,
Bide thou yet the tempest's shock."

    " Cold unrest and fasting,
    Life and strength are wasting,
Prithee, brother, let us halt ;
    Wherefore should we ever
    In this hard endeavour,
Waste our days on waves of salt ? "

H

" Brother, weak and errant,
 Seest thou not the current
Floats us back to frost and night;
 Self thou may'st not cherish,
 Here the slothful perish,
Onward to the land of light."

" Brother, all is changing,
 O'er the sea are ranging
Breezes from some blessed land ;
 Breezes odour-laden,
 Wafted from yon Aden,
High above the wave and sand.

Downy rest and leisure,
 Plenty, peace, and pleasure,
Yet shall crown our little lives ;
 Maids sweet songs shall sing us,
 And the years shall bring us
Friends and honours, homes and wives."

" Brother, go not thither,
 There the flowers all wither,
Spring hath there a poisoned breath ;
 Land of wailing lovers,
 Where each footfall covers
Offals of the feasts of death.

See ! where, ever vernal,
 Fields and flowers eternal
Bloom beneath the Father's eye ;
 There all storm and chillness
 End in sunny stillness,
Stillness of Eternity."

THE SKYLARK.

A T last I had a pleasant sleep,
  A sleep that brought once more to view
The pastures full of kine and sheep,
  And the old home my childhood knew.

The flowery bank on which I played
  All steeped in rainbow dyes appeared,
And mystical with light and shade
  The haunted woodland that I feared.

"And lo!" I said, "the brook still dashes,
  O'er rock and root and tumbled wall,
Into a thousand tinted flashes,
  Shiv'ring the sunbeams as they fall."

And soothingly the breeze that fann'd
  The heated schoolboy's throbing brow
Slid, softer than a sister's hand,
  O'er temples white with early snow.

Fainter than echoes to my ear
  Came sounds and voices, silent long—
A little brother's shout and cheer,
  The rustling reed and linnet's song.

My mother's humming wheel I heard,
 I heard her cheerful morning hymn,
And the brief prayer whose whispers stirred
 The crimson eventide hushed and dim.

Then eyes looked on me calm, serene,
 With love, love only in their beams—
Eyes closed and quenched, and to be seen
 No more for ever, save in dreams.

Upward, towards our Father's throne,
 The skylark climbed his spiral stairs,
And set to music of his own
 The praise that mingled with her prayers,

His song dispelled my later grief,
 I felt myself once more a boy,
And for a season, ah ! how brief,
 The heart grew glad with shadowy joy.

With happy tears my eyes were filled,
 And tears fell from them unawares ;
I woke, alas ! no more a child,
 But bowed and crushed with many cares.

The dear old home, the summer bloom
 Of field and woodland, all were gone ;
But near the window of my room
 A poor caged skylark warbled on.

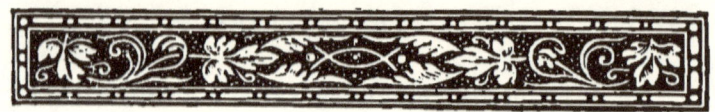

HOME.

MY home, my home, the very sound
　　Has raised the ready tear ;
Oh, should I roam the world around
　My heart would still be there.
I love my home, its hearth how dear,
The jewels of my soul are there.

Oh ! one can talk in accents meek
　Of days no more to come ;
Of moments when the changing cheek
Told all that language failed to speak—
　That loved one shares my home ;
Home, home shall be my pride and boast,
For those are there who love me most.

A fairy, gay and fresh and young,
　To grace that spot has come,
　The " Dada, dada," on her tongue,
Sweeter than aught a Sappho sung,
　Is music in my home.

Home, home, for me my heart knows not
A dearer, sweeter, happier spot,
Ah ! never may the fate be mine,
　In evil paths to roam,

Where wit and mirth, and song and wine,
Their pleasing sorceries combine,
  To draw me from my home.

Sorrow and toil, the poor man's fate,
In the rude world my steps await,
But bright'ning eyes and shout and glee,
And words of kindness, still shall be
  The welcome to my home.

My home, my home, the very sound
  Has raised the happy tear,
Oh should I range the world around,
  My heart would still be there.

THE OAK AND THE IVY.

'TWAS Springtime I saw them in beauty and pride,
   The Oak was a bridegroom, the Ivy a bride ;
Tall trees stood around them, some fairer than he,
But she twined round him only, so faithful was she.
No stranger with theirs mingled tendril or spray,
No neighbour might part them, so loving were they ;
Tho' slender the Ivy, how mighty the Oak,
The tempest, I ween, will be foiled in its stroke.

It was Winter I saw them 'mid trouble and strife,
The Oak was a husband, the Ivy a wife ;
The arms of the warrior were bared for the fight,
For whirlwinds rushed o'er him and storms in their might,
But he loved his own Ivy and stood to the last,
Tho' sudden the whirlwind and bitter the blast.

Then the frost like a serpent came after the storm,
But the Ivy's thick mantle was thrown o'er his form,
His branches the snow and the icicles bore,
But the cold of the winter wind touched not his core.
Thus lived they, thus bore they the trials of life,
The Oak was the husband, the Ivy the wife.

Again I beheld them, the tempest was nigh,
Yet proudly the Oak stood defying the sky,
The Ivy clung round him in thunder and rain,
But the bolt fell and ah! he was riven in twain;
In vain she weeps dewdrops, in vain twines around
The form of the loved one, to close up the wound.

His branches are blasted—all blackened his core,
The Ivy's a widow, the Oak is no more;
The Elm is beside her in beauty and pride,
Say, will she embrace him, once more be a bride,
Oh no, oh no, never, her leaves are all dim,
She has bloomed, she will fade, she will perish with him.

The Springtime returns and the forest is gay,
But the bride and the bridegroom, alas! where are they?
Oh, see where they slumber, the sere leaves beneath,
In life undivided, embracing in death.

PAUL ON THE HILL OF MARS.

CALM was the sea, the air, the hour,
   Yet from his lofty pedestal—
Dread type of human wrath and power—
The War-god fierce, implacable,
Frowned o'er the fearless Saint;
Fearless, yet fearing to offend;
Fearless, for ever to his ear
Came back the words that quelled all fear—
"Lo! I am with you to the end."

The sunlight beamed upon a brow
Calm as the seas that lay below,
And solemn as the skies above;
Peace, such as Stoics ne'er can know,
Was his, yet, quickened with the glow
Of purest, holiest love.
Amid the fanes—sublime abodes!—
And giant forms of chiselled stone,
The dauntless Hebrew stands alone,
True Titan! waring with the gods,
Even there, with deep, unfaltering tone.

The unknown Teacher, in the ear
Of cynic, priest, philosopher,

Proclaims the God unknown,—
The God in whom we live and move,
The eternal Light and Life and Love,
The first, the last, the part, the whole,
Creation's living heart and soul.
Oh ! Jupiter, sublime, supreme,
And art thou, sire of gods, become
At best a bard or sculptor's dream,
An idol, blind, and deaf, and dumb ?
Lo ! in the still, deserted fane,
The mourning priest is left alone,
The sea-nymph haunts no more the main,
The dryad from the grove is gone.
No bolt defends the thunderer's brow,
Vain, vain Apollo's wisdom now ;
No spirit in the statue dwells,
The fires die out, the oracles
Stammer and lie and cease.
Untired, unwasted, everywhere,
By fount, and grove, and sacred well,
In cities, and in isles afar,
The mighty Hebrew sounds the knell
Of all thy gods, O Greece.

ON THE DEATH OF RALPH GOODWIN.

SO the last meeting was indeed our last,
    And now in many a home and heart a place,
Silent and empty, shows that he has passed,
    To join the gathered fathers of his race.
    A thoughtful soul, whose gentleness and grace
Won love and honour; a true child of song,
    One in whose brief grand preludes we can trace
A tenderness and power, that might ere long
Have soothed a faithless grief, or lashed a sceptred wrong.

And dare we ask in wonder or in fear
    Why he is gone, and why we yet remain,
When conscience whispers in each inner ear
    " Vile culprit, thou that yet must drag the chain;
    Metal not half refined, that hath again
To pass the furnace, and endure its heat;
    Bird of weak wing, from which heaven's drenching rain
Must wash the mire of earth; soul all unmeet
To touch an angel's harp or listen at his feet."

Are we not captives in a strange weird land,
    Each manly frame a tower's enchanted walls?
Strong seems the pile to-day, but let the wand
    Of the grim wizard touch it, and it falls.

Oh ! for th' unshaken earth, th' eternal halls,
Where we may find a balm these wounds to heal,
  How long ! how long ! ere He, our Father, calls
To bid us don our robes and take our meal,
Where moth doth not corrupt, nor thieves break thro' and
    steal.

Sweet to the mortal, prone to unbelief,
  The treasured memories of the good and just ;
How like a star, in the black night of grief,
  Shines the clear truth, we are not wholly dust.
  The charnel holds among its worms and must
No attribute that man to man endears ;
  So out of sorrow comes a soothing trust,
And the soul cries, while soaring to the spheres,
" Mine ! mine ! these countless worlds ; mine ! mine ! th'
    eternal years."

THE BOTTLE IMP.

THE Bottle Imp smiled in his glassy retreat,
　　For a youth at the table had taken a seat,
　And surveyed the abode of the sprite ;
The liquor that sparkled and bubbled with life,
Was stirred by the demon of sorrow and strife,
　As he frisked in his impish delight.

" This solace the gods to the sufferer give,
When happy, 'tis then and then only we live,
　So drink," cried the Bottle Imp, " drink.
Life's sorrows are many, its pleasures are brief,
If sorrow oppress thee accept the relief,
　And cease for a season to think."

He took up the bottle and filled up the glass,
He shuddered and paused, and then drank, for, alas !
　A fiend of a tempter had he.
" In rags or in purple, in joy or in pain,"
He cried as he filled up the goblet again,
　" The bottle, the bottle for me."

A year passed away on its pinions unheard,
The victim again at the table appeared,
　But altered, without and within ;

His garments were tattered, his footsteps were slow,
His converse unseemly, the heart and the brow
   All dark with remorse and with sin.

" Drink deeply, for grief of the Bottle hath need,
Drink, drink," cried the Imp, " for thou know'st 'tis agreed
   Thy leisure and wages are mine ;
Thy youth, health, and beauty, thy purse and good name,
All these in exchange for my pleasures I claim,
   So drink," cried the spirit malign.

He drank, and the revel seemed joyous and wild ;
He sang, but the wail of his innocent child
   Oft rose o'er the bacchanal lay ;
And in spite of the bottle, a vision would come
Of the famishing wife, and the desolate home,
   Where slowly she wasted away.

Long after I saw that poor victim of wine,
A crime-spotted outcast, that mercy divine
   So long from perdition had screened ;
His aspect was savage, remorseless, and wild,
His bosom with hatred and envy was filled,
   The human was changed to the fiend.

" Grim famine has wasted thee e'en to the bone,
Thy health, reputation, and vigour are gone ;
   Poor coward, why fear'st thou the grave ?
A potion will poison, the dagger will kill,
The bags of a miser the bottle would fill,
   To be happy is but to be brave."

Thus whispered the tempter, and eagerly strode
The fiend-tempted fool on his errand of blood,
   As hurries the beast to his prey ;

Then horror and fear, and remorse and despair,
On his agonised features so terribly glare,
  That men start aback in dismay.

" There's peace in the bottle, a solace for all
The anguish and terror that man can appal,"
  The demon in ecstasy cried.
He ceased with a scoff, and the drunkard in haste
Snatched up the full bottle, and madly and fast
  Poured down the hot poison and died.

"Ah!" shouted the terrible spirit, " What joy,
What rapture to torture, to mar, and destroy!
  Can hell match the Imp of the Bowl?"
Poor drunkard, thy body lies senseless and stark,
On thee the foul tempter has finished his work,
  The Demon has captured the Soul.

LINES ON A DEAD INFANT.

AND art thou dead, indeed,
    Heaven's dearest, loveliest boon,
My babe, my sweet one, hast thou left
    Our home and arms so soon?

Saw'st thou what others wait
    For years and woes to prove,
The vanity and emptiness
    Of all that mortals love?

Or did some angel's voice
    Inform thy startled ear,
That wheresoe'er thy race is found,
    Sorrow and strife are there?

That life is but a dream,
    Alike to fool and sage,
With youth a morrow unenjoyed,
    A yesterday with age?

From things of earth and time,
    Thy flight has set us free,
To-day, our thoughts and hopes and hearts
    Are raised to heaven with thee.

Then let the tear be dried,
   For why should tears be shed?
Joy in thy heavenly home is found,
   Peace in thy earthly bed.

Can human thought conceive
   How great, how vast thy gain—
A whole eternity of bliss,
   Bought with a moment's pain?

Oh! Death, thy baffled sting
   Hath set thy victim free!
Look up, devouring Grave, and learn
   How poor thy victory!

A DEAD LETTER.

"THE lady, sir, at number two,
    The one that would not wed,
They say, sir, that at last she's gone,
    The poor old thing is dead."

Dead! dead! for me what deadly pain,
    What crowning agony;
How long within my breast had lain
    A hope that would not die.

Dead! dead! and is it so to be?
    Oh! soul, now saved and freed,
One word, look, moment, given to me,
    Had made me blest indeed!

"Sir, here's a letter, tied with string,
    And ticketed with care;"
It held a withered flower, a ring,
    A lock of braided hair.

"Dear James, I have not long to live,
    And fain would enter heaven,
My pride, my cruel pride forgive,
    Yours long has been forgiven.

"Oh! loved one, lost one, as I lie
    Wakeful upon my bed,
Some angel whispers, ' Do not die
    And leave the truth unsaid.'

"I know, I know, and grateful tears
    These closing eylids fill,
I know that thro' the weary years
    You loved, you blessed me still.

"So, lest one doubt should cause a sigh,
    Dear, faithful, wounded friend,
Know that thro' good and evil I
    Have loved thee to the end."

Slowly and grandly sinks the sun
    Behind yon far-off hill,
The long day's work will soon be done,
    And the tired world lie still.

My life, too, nears a golden west,
    But why should I despond ?
For me, true love and holy rest
    Lie treasured up beyond.

TO MY INFANT DAUGHTER.

COME kiss me, thing of smiles and mirth,
   Least earthly of the forms of earth,
Of all things fair and good below,
Most beautiful, most holy thou.
In depths of woe thy face appears,
Unmarred with anguish or with tears,
Lovely as summer skies when seen
Thro' the rent storm-cloud rolled between.
All sinless thou in depths of sin,
Angels thy playmates and thy kin,
A spirit gem, reflecting, even
In this dark world, the light of heaven.

How is't that childhood revels most
In joys that manhood long has lost ?
Oh ! there are charms for infant eyes
In birds and flowers, and fields and skies ;
What joy ! what rapture 'tis to view
The flower-lit green, the star-lit blue ;
Earth glows for them in Eden bloom,
All sunshine, beauty, song perfume.
Wouldst thou be happy, wouldst thou feel
The peace, the bliss, their looks reveal ?
Then pass not nature's volume by,
With hurried step and heedless eye ;

Babes can but read, where'er they look,
The preface of her wondrous book ;
But there are themes in every page
To please and teach the mind of age.

Wouldst thou be happy, free as they,
From cares that gnaw the heart away ?
Then let not burning lust of gain
The fount of holiest feelings drain,
Till peace, love, mercy, friendship, all
On the heart's desert blighted fall.
The kindly word, the kindly deed,
Belong thy brother in his need ;
Learn first to love, and thou shall taste,
Even in this world's unlovely waste,
The blessedness of those above—
For heaven is pure and perfect love.

LORD HENRY'S BRIDAL.

NO beast or bird to-night may sleep
    Near the Lord Henry's princely hall;
The far-off waters as they fall
In snow-sheets down yon rocky steep
Make music through the solemn hours;
The linnet in his garden bowers
Is lulled not by the slum'brous brook,
And vainly, vainly to and fro
The night-wind rocks the wakeful rook;
And, stealing from her reedy nook,
The swan in raiment white as snow
Sails ghost-like o'er the moonlit pool;
While, where yon elm trees, branching low,
Throw down their shadows dark and cool,
With lifted head and straining ear
Stand in still groups the wondering deer.

Lord Henry on that happy day
Had wed the Lady Angela.

A proud and high-born maiden she,
Whom love and wealth with sleepless care
Had shielded from each ruder air.
High-browed, pure-hearted, and so free
From trace of sin and care and toil,
So full of softness and of grace,

That while you gazed on form and face
You deemed her of some happier soil,
Some fair Elysium never yet
With drops of toil or sorrow wet.

A glorious being far above
The earth her aery footsteps spurned,
Whose presence changed desire to love
And love to adoration turned ;
The saint whose faith has scaled the skies,
And neared the inner golden door,
Hath seen her like in Paradise,
But never on this earth before.
And the Lord Henry was her own,
And the Lord Henry stood alone
On Fame's sublimest pedestal,
The buttress of a tottering throne,
The idol and the hope of all ;
The Titan swimmer whose strong hand   .
Buoyed up a weak and sinking land,
Saving, as God saves, friend and foe
From the black deep that boiled below.

'Twas meet the great man of the day
Should wed the Lady Angela.

So from afar the nobly born
Came to that old ancestral home,
And flute and hautboy, harp and horn,
Sent joy-notes to yon starry dome.
But all the while the fiends that mock
All human joy and hope and pain,
In dell and grove and haunted rock
Struck up anew each mirthful strain.

From many a fairy-trodden green,
And wooded hollow, dim and lone,
Came back each softened word or tone
Fron lips and instruments unseen—
A strange weird music soft and clear
Sounding like echoes to the ear.

Around the lighted halls there stood
The great ones of the passing times—
Grim warriors fresh from field and flood,
And potentates of many climes;
And mightier far the world's true kings
Who rule o'er human hearts, that bear
Their names and faces graven there;
These to their kind are purest springs,
With life, health, pleasure, brimming o'er;
Or spirit-suns that, fixed on high,
On generations born to die
Shed down their light for evermore.

And forms were there that seemed the bright
Inhabitants of other globes,
Whose fingers in their downward flight
Had wrought the rainbow into robes.
A queen among the queenly fair
Stood forth the Lady Angela;
No vesture gorgeously gay
Enshrined her form of purest mould,
No need had she of burnished gold,
Of tinted pearl or flashing gem,
The tresses of her shining hair
Her only crown and diadem.
She left the throng and stood apart,
And wept and sighed, yet knew not why,

Happy ! for from her closing eye
Tears of deep joy were quick to start.
Oh ! there are seasons when the heart
Is filled with all the love it craves,
For all our race a few brief hours
When we forget that earthly flowers
Are rooted in the soil of graves—
Hours when we dream that we are gods,
And fondly build eternal bowers
Even on this earth's once breathing clods.

But suddenly a startling cry
Rose in their midst from earth to sky—
A wild shrill cry, a rending shriek,
That sudden echoes sounded thrice—
A cry that whitened every cheek
And turned swift blood to stirless ice ; ·
And suddenly past lord and dame
Of spotless name and high descent
Strode a vile thing of guilt and shame,
In garb all travel-stained and rent—
A fierce-eyed spectre, white and worn,
That sought the great Lord Henry's seat,
And madly at his very feet
Cast down an infant, newly born.

Viol and harp and horn are mute,
The dancers paused with lifted foot,
And while the groups stood fixed as stone
The strange unbidden guest was gone.
Gone ! but the mad despair and ire,
The white arms skyward wildly tost,
Wrote her brief history as in fire—
Betrayed, forsaken, fallen, and lost.

There is a silence deep and dead
Where lately smiled the great and gay,
For rapid wheel and rushing steed
Have borne the revellers away ;
The last late lingering guest is gone,
And bride and bridegroom are alone.

Alas ! sweet soul, thou hast not dreamed
Thy sun could know such black eclipse—
That fruit which fresh from Eden seemed
Would turn to ashes on thy lips !
Foul sin hath placed a lasting bar
Between thy wedded lord and thee,
Henceforth your sundered hearts shall be
Like elements at chemic war,
That closely side by side may lie
Throughout a whole eternity,
Yet never like near dew drops run
To meet and lose themselves in one.

What ho ! thou proud and high-born lord,
Whose voice hath hushed a senate's hum,
What awful whisper hast thou heard
That youth and beauty strike thee dumb ?
Tell us, Lord Henry, why you sit
With troubled brow and quailing eye,
Like a black reptile of the pit,
That feels some strong archangel nigh ?
A blight hath touched *thy* ripened hope,
An ulcerous nakedness is thine,
The poison drop is in thy wine,
And Atè bids thee drink it up.
Lord Henry, thou shalt know to-day
That " as ye sow so shall ye reap,"

For vengeance like a beast of prey
Sleeps not, but only feigns to sleep.

There is another broken heart ;
Rise up, Lord Henry, and depart ;
Go, speechless, naked, and ashamed,
And take thy place among the damned.
Go, quickly, for thy lady's eyes,
So late with love's sweet moisture dim,
Flash like the swords of cherubim,
And wave thee out of Paradise.

Already Henry rues the day
He wed the Lady Angela.

ADELPHOS.

IT was the land, the brave old land,
  With warm and happy skies o'erspann'd,
And fragrant with Hymettus' breath;
The land of valour, art and song,
Where many a great soul, battling long,
Wrested a name from Time and Death;
There, ardent as the heavens above,
The young Adelphos woke to love.

As drinks Arabia's herbless sand
The night dew and the shower, his mind
Drank all the learning of his land,
Nor failed he in the end to find
The wisdom, mystical and grand,
Of Egypt and of hoary Ind,
Till his soul heard in caves or woods
The solemn whispers of the gods.

Still longing, yearning still to know,
He sought the porch where sages sate,
And as he journeyed to and fro
The youth, O Phidias, passed thy gate,
And there, all lighted with the glow
Of sunset, he, returning late,
Saw near the open lattice shine,
Fair as the moon, a face divine.

Then died the thirst for hidden lore
That, night and day, his soul possessed;
Sighing, he whispered evermore,
" 'Tis love, not knowledge, makes us blest;
'Tis love that when the heart is sore
Breathes o'er it an Elysian rest;
Not in the dim and silent cell
Of the lone sage does solace dwell."

To islands rich in flowers and fruits
He sails o'er shining ocean streams,
And there in thought he roams, as suits
His fancy, lulled to blissful dreams
By music from Arcadian lutes;
Or, 'neath the shade of spicy groves,
Clasps to his heart the maid he loves.

Once more 'twas eventide, once more
The student neared the sculptor's home,
There stood all glorious as before
The fairest 'neath that starry dome,
While eyes that to his spirit bore
A heaven of joy and hope said " Come."
Filled with a bliss before unknown,
The youth drew near and clasped—a stone.

Statue of Pallas! Maid divine!
How calm! how pure thy marble brow!
Poor youth! with that first touch of thine
Love and love's happy visions go,
And never more on thee will shine
Aught human that can heal thy woe;
Earth hath not—earth shall never see—
Such heavenly grace and purity.

TO A FRIEND IN DISTRESS.

THY secret wound with patience bear,
  'Tis great to suffer as to do,
And souls that wrestle with despair,
  And wrestle nobly, vanquish too :
The ivy, buried by the fall
Of ruined arch, or crumbling wall,
  Puts forth anew its little might
  And strains and struggles for the light,
Its crushed and broken tendrils slow
  Through dark and rugged windings run,
Upward, and upward still, and lo !
  At last they revel in the sun ;
So, souls that climb with patient strength
  From depths of anguish or despair,
Shall, step by step, attain at length
  A nobler life, a purer air.

A CHRISTMAS HYMN.

"GLORY to God, and peace on earth,"
      In heaven the hymn began,
And angels rushed, like falling stars,
      To sing the words to man.

"Glory to God, and peace on earth,"
      The Son of Man replied;
His solitary voice was hushed,
      He prayed, and wept, and died.

"Glory to God, and peace on earth,"
      The anthem peals again;
Earth's wildest discords cannot drown
      That one celestial strain.

Hark! far and near th' undying words
      From human lips are given,
'Mid tears and chains, and blood and fire,
      They soar from earth to heaven.

"Glory to God, and peace on earth,"
      Thro' ages dark and long,
Earth's noblest, wisest, holiest sons
      Have sung th' immortal song.

Riches and power are vain, and vain
　　The lore of cherubim,
For tears shall flow, and hearts shall bleed,
　　Till man shall learn the hymn.

THE LAST MAN.

THE wigwam to the ground was burned,
   The buffalo and moose were gone,
So sire and son arose and turned
   Towards the setting sun.

Long, long they journeyed, sore beset
   By wild beasts and by wilder men,
And after saddest farewells met
   Unslaughtered once again.

At last they came where never foot
   The low, dark, wooded gorge had trod,
And deep within the desert shut
   They dwelt alone with God.

There, mourning o'er their slaughtered braves,
   They sat beside their fire and wept;
Alas! how distant from the graves
   Where their dead fathers slept.

But time dried up their tears, they dreamed
   No more of ambush, fray, or wound;
The vale so still, so peaceful, seemed
   A blessed hunting ground.

K

Oft in the still night, all unheard,
  Save by the listening ears beneath,
The Spirit-Father came and stirred
  The pine-tops with his breath.

But slowly to that happy dell
  The pale-face followed on their tracks ;
Hark ! hark ! again the red man's knell,
  The rifle and the axe.

The dark-eyed hunters of the vale
  Went forth to fight their Christian foe ;
But vain against the leaden hail
  The hatchet and the bow.

The father's tearless eyes beheld
  His sole son hid beneath the clay ;
He lived to see his forests felled,
  His wigwam swept away.

A pine tree, charred and leafless, rose
  Above the whiteman's fields of corn,
And there the man of many woes
  Oft stood in mood forlorn.

And when the axeman sought that spot,
  The chief stood by with frenzied air ;
He spoke not, stirred not, heeded not
  The cry " Beware ! beware ! "

So, there they lie in mire and blood
  Like lovers locked in fond embrace—
The last tree of the primal wood,
  The last man of his race.

SONG.

OH! tell me not that we must part—
 That may not, cannot be,
For distance never can divide
 Two beings such as we.

No, we shall live in bye-gone hours—
 Hours we can ne'er forget—
And nightly in our visions meet,
 As we have often met.

To know that happiness is thine
 My sum of bliss shall be,
I ne'er shall know what sorrow is
 If evil harm not thee.

Hope pointed once to coming years
 All radiant with her light,
But now the future fades in gloom,
 The past alone is bright.

Then let us live in bye-gone hours—
 Hours we can ne'er forget—
And nightly in our visions meet,
 As we have often met.

THE BETRAYER.

HE let not darkness hide him,
　　But sought the festive throng;
Frail beauty sat beside him
　　To charm with mirth and song.

He braved the dread hereafter,
　　He joined the joyous band,
And held amid the laughter
　　The wine cup in his hand.

Yet oh! had ye but seen him,
　　But seen the stare—the start,
There was no mirth within him,
　　No sunshine on his heart.

He left them with their gladness,
　　He found not what he sought,
He hoped in bacchant madness
　　To end the hell of thought.

Abroad, the stars above him,
　　Earth, ocean, all we see,
Find language to reprove him,
　　And whisper, " Where is she ? "

THE BETRAYER. 133

His tongue of love hath spoken,
  Hath uttered vows in guile,
A heart, a heart is broken,
  He doth not, cannot smile.

She cursed him? Oh, no never
  Reproached him? but with tears,
Alas! for him, she ever
  Hath named him in her prayers.

She heart for heart could render,
  Her wish was but to bless,
Her nature was all tender,
  Her sin was love's excess.

Alone or 'mid the revel,
  On land or on the sea,
Alike the accusing devil
  Will whisper, " Where is she?"

His tongue of love hath spoken,
  Hath uttered vows in guile,
A heart, a heart is broken,
  He doth not, shall not smile.

TO MY WIFE, WITH MY PORTRAIT.

LOVED as maiden, wooed as bride,
   Proved in storm, in sunshine tried,
Near me in life's battle stand,
Balm for wounds in either hand.

Mine, while heart and pulse shall move,
Mine, mine only be thy love—
Love that in the darkest day
Knows no limit, no decay;

Love that screens with sainted kiss
Sin-spots dark as Eblis is ;
Love that in fair hues can dress
Even mine own unworthiness.

Time-worn hollows now entomb
Vanished youth and faded bloom,
Yet, oh yet, beloved one,
Mourn not youth and beauty gone.

Onward let the seasons move,
Years but ripen faithful love,
Here as ever may'st thou see
Eyes that draw their light from thee,

Lips that evermore the same
Breathe their blessings on thy name,
Bosom broad that holds beneath,
Love too strong for time and death—

Bosom broad, that, bared, could show
Depths of love thou ne'er canst know—
Bosom broad, that, deep within,
Holds a heart fast knit to thine—

Heart that singeth night and day
Thee, thee only, thee for aye,
Happy heart! song ceasing never,
Thee, thee only, thee for ever.

SONG OF THE VOLUNTEERS.

CANNON'S lightning flash and thunder,
  Steel and ball, delight not us,
Not for glory, not for plunder,
  Arm we like the Celt or Russ.

Wolfish troops of cruel spoilers
  Flit like shadows round our store,
England's sleepless angel whispers
  Loose the watch-dog, bolt the door.

Sweat and blood of sage and warrior
  Bought our charters, one by one,
Shall we sleep, and find on waking
  All our wealth of freedom gone?

By our hate of chains and darkness,
  Never here while hearts are brave
Priest shall mock the shade of Cromwell,
  Tyrant spit on Milton's grave.

Round the bones of bard and hero,
  Round the altar, fold, and flock,
Rifles! in the hour of danger,
  Rise like walls of living rock.

Oh! should banded slave and despot
  Taint the soil that Hampden trod,
Rifles! let a storm of bullets
  Blast them like the wrath of God.

When, unfettered, beast and devil
  Seek in homes of peace their prey,
Mercy dons the helm of valour,
  Crying " Freemen, up and slay."

FIRST LOVE.

WE spake not, for we could not speak,
    So great the doubt—the fear,
But earnest eye conversed with eye,
    And pleading tear with tear ;
Ah! oft in silent tears we mourn
The love in tears and silence born.

Her trembling form was clasped to mine
    In love's delightful fold,
While beating heart to beating heart
    Its mighty yearnings told,
The doubt was passed—the fear was gone,
Th' unutterable secret known.

A rapture never felt before
    Thro' all my being stole,
For heart was then dissolved in heart,
    And soul was lost in soul ;
What joy such joy but to receive,
What blessedness such bliss to give !

The waters of a gushing spring
    O'er the heart's desert ran ;
That hour another world was made,
    Another life began, .
An inner world—apart from this,
A life of unimagined bliss.

Our meetings were life's holidays,
　From toil and sorrow won,
They gave a sweetness to the flower,
　A brightness to the sun;
Earth with the tints of Eden glowed,
All bright and beautiful and good.

Love was a seraph's harpings heard
　Above earth's din and strife,
A strain of heavenly poesy
　Amid the prose of life,
Bidding from hallowed soul and heart
All sorrow and all sin depart.

'Tis gone, the sunshine of my years,
　The first gleam and the last,
In sorrow, hope and memory view
　The future and the past;
'Tis gone, and there are left for me
A darkened sky, a shoreless sea.

'Tis gone, that earnest, holy love,
　Too pure, too bright to last,
But it has left the loneliness,
　The hunger, and the waste;
In silence and in tears I mourn
The love in tears and silence born.

THE FETTERED TO THE FREE.

SON of Earth, revisit earth thy primal home,
   Hither, hither, hither, spirit brother, come;
Things of earth no longer fill my pургèd core,
Eyes that once have seen thee look to earth no more.
Shine, O radiant spirit, shine on me from far,
As when dies the daylight shines the hidden star;
Faint, remote, and feeble is the young lark's cry,
Yet how soon it bringeth kindred from the sky.
Come, then, bright immortal, from thy starry home,
Hither, hither, hither, Son of Glory, come;
Gleams afar thy pinion, shines thy face at last,
Let the mystic slumber seal my senses fast.
Lo, Thy touch hath freed me, loosed me from the clay,
Onward, spirit, onward, upward, and away.
Away, away, as the wild bird springs
On high, on high, when its bounding wings
Have burst from the broken snare;
Away, away, with the Son of Light,
O'er the snowy cloud and the mountain's height,
Away to yon peopled star;
Away, away, thro' the boundless blue,
Unseen, unheard, like the morning dew—
The dew that stayed but a transient hour
On the lowly grass or the queenly flower,
Too pure for the earth and bright;

Away, where night with her robe of gloom
Never hath been and never shall come ;
Away, away, where the star-beam flings
Its rainbow-dyes on the aery wings
That wave in its holy light.
The bird shall stoop to its leafy bower,
The dew shall fall in a summer shower
And again make the earth look gay,
But the happy soul to the stars shall rise,
And wonder and love shall glow in its eyes,
While the ages as days pass away.

THE POET.

THE poet stands in solemn mood
 Amid the whisp'ring solitude ;
The stars that girl the far-off pole
Speak to his list'ning earnest soul ;
The night-wind and the ocean's roar
Utter their deep and solemn lore ;
To him, all forms in mystic speech
Lessons of priceless wisdom teach,
He only can their whispers hear,
He, Nature's own interpreter.

'Tho' oft' unheard, or heard amiss,
Still, still for him creation is
Heaven's language, God's unchanging word,
By night, by day, for ever heard—
Heard as when first the measured chime
Of moving worlds gave birth to time—
Voices which, heeded or unheard,
Shall yet speak out till time shall be
Gone, like a night-toll, that but stirred
The stillness of eternity.

Alas ! that poet ever strove
To wake the throb of guilty love,
Alas ! that e'er the sacred lyre
Was touched to rouse the warrior's ire,

That sounds so heavenly e'er should be
Blended with bacchant revelry.

Not so, sings God and Nature's bard,
Heaven and not fame is his reward;
His are the songs whose numbers roll
Their gusts of feeling o'er the soul,
Stirring its deeps as breezes wake
To life and health the stagnant lake;
His are the strains that soothe to rest
The furies of the human breast,
Flood the dark soul with light, and dart
Like sunbeams through the frozen heart;
His spoken music, even when wild
As is the wildest minstrelsy
Of rushing wind or roaring sea,
With trumpet notes of truth is filled—
A music bringing peace, and hopes
Of power to calm remorse and fear.

Yet, sweet and holy as the tear,
The first tear a fond mother drops
O'er the still babe that slumbers near,
His words, with fire celestial fraught,
Quicken the buried seeds of thought—
God planted seeds that, as they shoot
Upward into the daylight, grace
With beauty, verdure, flowers, and fruit
The dreary mental wilderness.

Comes to his ear the word divine,
From all below, around, above,
He sees without, he feels within,
The eternal Life, and Light, and Love;

And God's own language, whispered long,
Bursts from his lips in fervid song—
Song that shall sound in human ears
His changeless truth thro' changing years.

REQUIEM.

ROUND her they gather,
        Lover, friend, father,
Mournfully gazing on beauty's low bed,
        Airs known in childhood,
        Sounding thro' wild wood,
Melt not the soul like the hymn for the dead.

        Wild birds are singing,
        Breezes are bringing
Fragrance and music from flower and from tree,
        Earth in her gladness
        Heeds not thy sadness,
Mourns not, and joys not, O mortal, with thee.

        Joyously o'er us
        Rises the chorus,
Beauty and life fill the field and the sky,
        Blithe, but it cheers not,
        Loud, tho' she hears not,
Lovely as Eden, tho' darkened her eye.

        Graves, deep and hollow,
        Ope, and we follow,
On to the home where our fathers abide,
        Yet fear not and weep not,
        For spirits that sleep not
Wait at the portal to welcome and guide.

L

Rise, O young spirit,
Rise and inherit
Regions unsaddened by death and decay,
Sisters that love thee
Hover above thee,
Look not behind thee, but shorten their stay.

THE SABBATH.

REST, child of Adam, rest,
  Thy couch in quiet keep,
To-day no sound unblest
  Shall break thy happy sleep,
To-day the Sabbath brings for thee
Its brief but welcome jubilee.

Sad, sad thy portion here,
  For oft unseen of all
The sweat-drop and the tear
  To earth in silence fall ;
Then rest, poor slave, thy wasted frame,
These hours stern Mammon dares not claim.

Sorrow and toil have marred
  The form and " face divine,"
For labours long and hard
  And woes unnamed are thine ;
So rest the aching heart and head,
To-day an angel guards thy bed.

One blessed day in seven,
  O toiler, mean and poor,
An unseen hand from heaven
  Throws wide thy prison door,
And bending Mercy—even to thee,
Poor child of Adam—saith, " Be free."

Tho' low and mean thy state,
　　And tho' thy portion be
Scorned of the rich and great,
　　A God remembers thee ;
Tho' stained and marred, and sin-defiled,
The world's great Father owns his child.

These hours from Mammon's grasp
　　His thoughtful mercies wrest,
That toil in peace may clasp
　　His darlings to his breast,
That wife and babes may round him come
Within his oft-forsaken home.

The flow'ret's folded cup
　　Opes in the morning ray,
The glorious sun is up,
　　It shines for thee to-day,
To-day for thee the stream shall flow,
The wild bird sing, the zephyr blow.

Come quickly, gladly come,
　　From scenes of toil and guilt ;
Come, see the radiant home
　　Our Father's hand hath built,
In the warm sun, on earth's green sod,
The soul best sees, most loves, her God.

While soul and heart shall live,
　　Thro' toil, and wrong, and ill,
Strain, mortal, strain and strive
　　Upward, and upward still ;
Strain, for there is a rest on high—
The Sabbath of eternity.

To-day the loosened chain,
   Th' unfettered thought and limb,
The truce to care and pain,
   Shall prompt the thankful hymn ;
Break into songs of holy mirth,
For heaven to-day comes down to earth.

NIGHT THOUGHTS.

THE midnight's thick and heavy gloom
  Fell sadly, sadly as the heap
On the last bed where mortals sleep,
While Nature, hid as in a tomb,
Awaited light and life's return,
The resurrection of the morn.

Flowers, sunshine, beauty, all had gone,
Had vanished, and I was alone,
Alone! alone! no sound or sight
The straining ear or eye to bless,
Methought that all things fair and bright
Had fallen again to nothingness;
Alone! alone! I seemed to be
A shipwreck of infinity.

But solitude and darkness brought
An hour with awful musings fraught;
Oh there are deep, still moments when
The bottom of our hearts is seen,
And there's a voice we never hear
In the rude world's unholy din—
A voice that speaks not to the ear,
But ghost-like comes when none are near,
And whispers to the soul within.

It speaks, we look around and see
That all things dear and fond and fair,
That hope had said would bless us, bear
Death's sad inscription, " Vanity."

That voice, that whisper of heaven's love,
Oft comes to warn, instruct, reprove,
It speaks of buried friends, of eyes
Whose light we never more may see,
Of what we are and yet may be,
Of life, of death, of mysteries,
Sad, solemn, terrible, sublime ;
It bids us from the brink of time
Look onward to eternity—
That crumbling brink from which the day,
The hour, the moment, slide away
To melt like snowflakes in that sea,
Dark, shoreless, bottomless, unknown,
Where all our yesterdays are gone.

How good it is to steal an hour
From sleep, and close the weary eyes
On earth's gay nothings in disguise.
A setting sun, a faded flower,
The wail of brook or breeze, has power
To speak a wisdom to the heart
That tongue or pen can ne'er impart.
The mystic voice that comes from hill,
Grove, lake, or insect-peopled sod,
When all without, within, is still,
Is Nature's voice, the voice of God.

THE OLDEN DAYS.

COME, memory, unbind thy written scroll,
　　Show me thy treasured pictures, one by one,
My path grows dark and lonely, and my soul
Would fain look back on years and loved ones gone.
Restore, if but in dreams, the light that shone
On the first home my happy childhood knew ;
Those pleasant spots I fain would look upon,
And thou alone canst give them to my view,
For time hath changed and marred what time can ne'er
　　renew.

Far off and faint as echoed echoes, comes
Back to my ears a streamlet's bubbling flow,
While bathed in sunshine rise three cottage homes,
And close beside a farmstead, grey and low ;
A grove lies eastward, to the west a brow
Slopes gently down to pastures broad and green,
Whence glances here and there the brook's unresting
　　sheen.

On the green walls that gird that quiet spot
The bright-eyed robin shows his crimson vest,
And 'neath the lowly eaves of barn and cot
The dainty swallow builds her rustic nest ;
When, crowned with flowers, with fragrant winds
　　caress'd,

O'er melting snows first came the dancing Spring,
From deepest glen to mountain's wooded crest
Joy spake in song, while larks, on circling wing,
Made the far realm of clouds with love's own music ring.

I love ye still, ye kindly, homely folks,
Peopling the world that perished long ago ;
There, side by side, ye stand, like forest oaks,
Shielding each other while the tempests blow.
Of this world's wisdom little do ye know,
Nor do ye love its hard and selfish creed ;
It is your daily wont in prayer to bow,
And how shall souls that cry " Our Father " breed
Strife among brethren, or forget a brother's need ?

The ploughshare glitters in the morning sun,
And young and old their cheery tasks resume,
Abroad, o'er broken fields the harrows run,
At home, the maidens ply the wheel and loom.
No envious mood, no dumb, unthankful gloom,
Darkens the happy sunshine of the heart ;
Toil is their lot, but not severe their doom,
For health and healthful sleep their toils impart,
And love is ever near to soothe misfortune's smart.

Fair these retreats, but fairer still to me
The human forms that bless my dreamy gaze,
Dearer than hearth or homestead, brook or tree,
The kind, good people of the olden days.
But ah ! the aery scene no longer stays,
My early friends in vain by name I call,
I tread on withered leaves, my spirit strays
Weeping thro' a lost Eden, where the Fall,
Like a down-rushing storm, hath marred and ruined all.

THREE LITTLE BROTHERS:

A NURSERY RHYME.

THREE little brothers, all pretty and good,
   Once had a nice little home in a wood,
    And father and mother,
    For these and no other,
Worked in the long day as hard as they could.

Father, before he went out in the day,
Smiling, would turn to the darlings and say,
    " You must stop in the house
    And be still as a mouse,
Lest you be stolen when we are away.

" Little ones, mind and do just as you're bid—
Mosses quite cover your house like a lid,
    And so thickly o'erhead
    The branches are spread,
Robbers may never know where you are hid."

Oh ! many a bright summer day in that year,
The babes with their father and mother were there,
    And they grew before long
    To be healthy and strong,
And beautiful garments were given them to wear.

But it happened one day, when the parents were out,
That they said to themselves, "There's no danger
    about,
  So as nobody sees
  We will climb up the trees,
And for once in our lives have a laugh and a shout."

Just then a giant had entered the wood,
Looking for berries or other such food,
  And he heard them while walking,
  All laughing and talking,
And in a moment before them he stood.

The poor little brothers all jumped into bed,
And each did his utmost to cover his head;
  But he tore down their home—
  From foundation to dome—
And bore off the brothers all trembling with dread.

To keep them alive in a prison he tried,
And scolded and beat them whenever they cried;
  So they strove all their might
  To escape in the night,
And finding they could not they lay down and died.

Those three little brothers were birds in one nest;
The giant and robber that killed them in jest
  Was a boy you know well,
  But his name I wont tell,
Tho' he sits in the nook, with his chin on his breast.

ON WAR.

EVER, O Earth, thy rolling sphere
    Hangs midway between heaven and hell,
The bourne of unseen kingdoms, where
    The angel and the demon dwell;
Where good and evil, night and day,
O'er all things hold divided sway.

For ever thro' the infinite,
    Earth moves among the orbs; her form
Half bathed in darkness, half in light,
    Her glory stained with cloud and storm;
The fate of all of earthly race
Thus mirrored in her changing face.

Earth never new the reign of love,
    The sway of just and holy law,
Since Time began the bleeding dove
    Has writhed beneath the falcon's claw;
For here the gods have built no fence
Around the home of innocence.

Earth's face is one wide battle-field,
    Marred with the stains and wrecks of strife,
The combats of the wood and wild
    But types of man's sublimer life,
For man, too, joins the mighty war
In which all lesser beings share.

Iu every age the undying Goth
   Has wrestled with th' eternal Rome ;
The Furies gather in their wrath,
   Where'er the Graces build a home ;
And oceans, cold and dark and deep,
Wait, watch, and hunger for the ship.

Dread forces, bidding mountains reel,
   Vesuvia's verdure oft has screened,
And oft beneath the angel's heel
   Lies, as tho' dead, th' immortal fiend.
Ah ! fire and fiend too oft have driven
Pale Peace to her sole home in heaven.

A SIGH.

FAIR as an infant's laughing face
    The world around me seems,
An Eden filled with forms of grace,
Where Love might find a resting-place
    And live out all his dreams.

A listening, momentary calm
    O'er all the landscape broods;
Then breezes, bringing health and balm,
Sing, soft and low, a holy psalm
    Through gently swaying woods.

Yet this is not the home of Love,
    But one wide scene of strife;
Yon hawk o'erhangs the cooing dove,
And here all living things must prove
    The bitterness of life.

And human hearts oft pine for ease,
    In Summer's greenest bowers,
And grief will come, where all should please,
Sighs blend with heaven's delightful breeze,
    And tears descend on flowers!

ON THE NEW YEAR.

RUSHING years but leave behind them
    Waning strength and failing breath,
Heart and pulse, O mortal, ever
    Time the tread of coming Death.

One by one the loosened moments
    Drop into the gulf below,
Heart and pulse are but an echo
    Of the miner's ceaseless blow.

While we slumber, while we trifle,
    Evermore Time works our fall,
Solemn thought, that, like a spectre,
    Comes to startle and appal.

Give we then to noblest labours
    Youthful years and manhood's prime,
So our deeds shall stand for ever,
    Rocks amid the stream of Time.

Be our strife for truth and wisdom,
    For the world, the life to come,
Aery earth hath no foundation
    For the spirit's lasting home.

Let the tongue and life have fruitage,
   Words and deeds of purest love,
Mindful of the place we stand on—
   Graves beneath us, God above.

Shall great souls that heard the "Well done,"
   Mortals risen to high estate,
See the searcher at the portal
   Turn us from the golden gate?

Earth is full of wrong and evil,
   Vast our work and brief our space,
Up then, brother, and in earnest
   Fight the battle, run the race.

Let us cleanse the inner temple,
   Let us live before we die,
That, when naked, we may blushless,
   Meet the angels eye to eye.

Whether called to dare or suffer,
   Valiant, patient, let us prove,
Knights, true knights of God's first order,
   All mankind our lady-love.

THE MYSTIC VOYAGE.

WE loved, for side by side we grew together,
  And many a summer day from noon till even
We sat and talked upon the moorland heather,
  Till earth grew fairer than our dreams of heaven.

But one sad morn the last long breathless slumber
  Came, and she rose not from her fixed repose;
For she was added to the favoured number
  That rise from earth ere they have known its woes.

Her grave but held an empty husk, yet near it
  Hours sad and many have I sate and wept;
But once while there deep peace came o'er my spirit,
  Like stillness on the noontide, and I slept.

And in that sleep, as if from sleep awaking,
  I saw my Mary seated at my side;
Around the bark in which we sate were breaking
  The wide waste waters of an ocean tide.

Swift was the stream whose waves had borne us thither,
  And doubt and peril filled our hearts with fear,
For whence we came we knew not—knew not whither
  That rushing flood our tiny bark would bear.

M

And many a fireless hearth and roofless dwelling
　Rose o'er the broad and undulating tide,
And many a dome and sunlit temple telling
　Of gods and nations that had lived and died.

And oft our hearts grew faint with vain endeavour
　To reach far islands, wondrous green and fair,
Where love would fain have made his home for ever,
　That as we neared them melted into air.

At last, when many weary days were ended,
　And many perils, many woes were past,
From the far sky an awful night descended,
　As chaos beamless, and as chaos vast.

Still onward, o'er the waters wide and trackless,
　Our little vessel glided silently,
Still onward, tho' the huge and heavy blackness
　Rose like a solid wall from sea to sky.

And there, amid the darkness and the stillness,
　Strange fire-eyed phantoms made us start and shrink,
And o'er our bodies crept a mortal chillness,
　As inch by inch our boats began to sink.

But in that hour of darkness and of terror,
　Two angels suddenly appeared in sight,
And the black deep reflected like a mirror,
　Those radiant forms, twin stars of sorrow's night.

One near my sainted Mary loved to linger,
　Whose low, soft whispers woke a happy smile,
And one, with straining eye and lifted finger,
　Looked as it seemed to some yet hidden isle.

Headlong at last our wave-worn barque descended
   Down to black deeps to rot with wreck and sand,
But o'er their charge those strong twin angels bended,
   And wings upbore us to an unknown land.

How sweet it was to hear the soft wind sighing
   Thro' the green bowers on Eden's shining coast,
How sweet to hear long silent voices crying
   "They come! they come! the loved ones we had lost."

I woke; the drowning maid—the weary billow—
   The dwellers in the far-off spirit spheres,
All, all had vanished, but the stony pillow
   Whereon I lay was wet with happy tears.

HYMN.

FATHER, full of tender mercies,
   Thou alone our God shalt be,
Long, too long, our feet have wandered
   Far from happiness and Thee.

Doubt and dread and sin and sorrow,
   Haunt us still whene'er we roam,
Father, keep us ever near Thee,
   Safely guide and guard us home.

Father, we are blind and feeble,
   Stumbling on in fear and pain,
Let Thy truth our path illumine,
   Let Thy love our feet sustain.

Father, we are weak and weary,
   Here we toil and watch and weep,
Gently take us to Thy bosom,
   Give to Thy beloved—sleep.

THE SWALLOW.

A FABLE.

NO longer sought the sportive fly
    The azure of the summer sky,
For winds ungentle day by day
Snatched from the stem the whirling spray,
And chilling fogs, like sheets of lead,
Hung o'er the mown and withered mead.
'Twas then, well screened from cold and wet,
The birds in solemn council met ;
The grey old steeple ere its fall
Became a senatorial hall,
Where feathered statesmen, small and great,
Discussed at ease affairs of state.
The strong, as often is the case
With strong ones of a higher race,
Shed tears while gazing on the weak ;
To shattered wing and broken beak
They spake of over-population,
And recommended emigration.
But one rose up, when all was still,
And, wiping his melodious bill,
Addressed, in deep and earnest words,
That multitude of listening birds—
" My friends, I should have longer sate
To hear your wisdom in debate,

But that I oft have heard within
The whispers of a voice divine,
It comes I know not whence or why,
But I must either speak or die.
It tells me that a winter comes,
Whose tempest will destroy our homes,
And, what is worse, exterminate
The tribes which now our hunger sate;
But there are lands beyond the main,
Where summer holds her sunny reign,
Of dearth, of cold, we need not die,
For thither yet we all may fly,
As heaven will send us helpful gales
To waft us to those blessed vales."
Each feathered hearer heard within
An echo of the voice divine,
And all while listening to the youth
Felt for the time the power of truth,
And fearless of the frowning skies
Raised the wild cry " Arise, arise."
But ere the crowd could upward spring,
With hopeful heart and straining wing,
A wit and scholar pert and gay
Just hinted he'd a word to say;
This bird had worshipped thro' the season
The goddess called by students Reason.
A knowing bird in sooth was he,
As ever perched on barn or tree,
For he to life and light was brought
Where laws and languages are taught,
And in his nest for weeks had sate
Listening to doctors in debate,
Till he, like them, had gained a store
Of useless metaphysic lore.

Few grey professors of the college
Knew more than he of God's foreknowledge,
Or chattered more familiarly
Of free-will and necessity.
On lengthy arguments he'd enter
To prove a circle had no centre,
For well knew he, with learned rules
To mystify unlettered fools,
And floor with quibble, wit, pretence,
That clumsy giant, common sense.
" That speaker, friends," said he, " I wist
Is but a canting Methodist,
Since he exhorts you one and all
T'obey some fancied inward call ;
Or he may be (the godless rogue)
A poor but crafty demagogue,
That, discontented with his state,
Would ruin nations to be great,
Or—ay—his very features show it,
A wild-eyed, ranting, crack-brained poet.
'Tis true our fathers gave command
That we should leave this stricken land
As soon as we had strength to brave
A journey o'er the endless wave,
But they have sent their children dear
No known and trusty messenger,
To tell us of their happy lot,
In the far land where they are—not.
My friend the redbreast holds 'tis clear
'Tis possible to winter here,
And in my neighbour's word I trust,
Let others go, if go they must.
The fish that ate their fathers will
Devour them to the claws and bill,

But when those epicures you see,
Just say they need not wait for me."
They heard but heeded not, and fast
Rose upward on the rushing blast,
While full of self-conceit and pride
The babe of reason stayed—and died.

DIRGE.

AH ! how shall tongue or pen express
   The loneliness and pain,
When hearts, that long have beat as one,
   By death are rent in twain.

Yet joys most holy have their birth
   In sorrow's darkest hours,
As rainbows light with glorious hues
   The gloom that ends in showers.

When daylight dies, the shining veil
   From starry worlds is riven,
So griefs that darken earthly hopes
   Give brighter views of heaven.

My love, my husband, thou art there,
   Thou smil'st on me from far,
As on the lone, lost mariner
   Looks down the steadfast star.

Sweet thoughts of thee, my sainted lord,
   My guiding light shall be,
That thro' the mists and storms of time
   Shall draw my soul to thee.

THE DEMONS' CHASE.

UNSEEN, unheard, in silent air
    We wander night and day ;
We dig the pitfalls, spread the snare,
    The lures in order lay.

We haunt the couch, the hearth, the mart,
    We follow everywhere,
Unfelt, yet brooding o'er the heart,
    Unknown, yet ever near.

No trembling beast we chase, or bird,
    In river, brake, or tree,
But night and day, unseen, unheard,
    The soul, the soul hunt we.

Softly, softly, youth lies yonder,
    Passion's sigh perfumes the gale ;
How his eyes, with love and wonder,
    Gaze on beauty, false and frail.

Fair is woman, fair is ocean
    When the weary whirlwind sleeps,
Let no plash, no fierce emotion,
    Tell what monsters crowd their deeps.

Shades and silence aid temptation,
  Imps the young delusion nurse;
Lo! he wooes the sweet damnation,
  Panting, clasps the smiling curse.

Dig the pitfall, spread the net,
  Courage! we shall have him yet;
Hark! amid the festive throng,
  Flushed with wine, he sings the song—

" Youth is life's holiday, sunny and bright,
  Catch from the moment the flying delight;
Drain the full goblet, right joyously sing—
  Pleasure is mortal, and Time hath his wing;
Live while ye live, and rejoice while ye may,
  Life is a lamp, ever wasting away."

Echo the chorus, ye imps, as ye glance
Arrow-like on o'er the whirls of the dance;
Spread the dark wing, lest a sunbeam from heaven
Show him the pitfall to which he is driven;
Prompt the lewd song, lest the spirits above
Startle his soul with a whisper of love;
See that young roses, the fair and the sweet,
Hide the deep hell that is under his feet.

See him in that earnest crowd,
  Ripe in manhood, stern and proud;
Wine, and song, and mirth are o'er,
  Woman falls, to reign no more;
Woman falls, but in their turn
  Other lusts within him burn;
Dig the pitfall, spread the net,
  Courage! we shall win him yet."

Rise, Son of Glory, and go forth,
  With guns and swords and spears,
Manure the oft polluted earth
  With ashes, blood, and tears.

The bright green bay shall be thy meed,
  Thy name shall fill all lands,
Earth shall applaud each glorious deed,
  And hell shall clap her hands.

Or, with the statesman's subtle toils,
  Bind struggling freedom down,
Fill all thy palaces with spoils,
  For none but God will frown.

The vanities of manhood, Age
  Beholds with pity or with sneers;
" Gold !" cries the wisdom of the sage,
  " Gold !" cries the fool of many years.

Heedless of mis'ry, firm and fast
  Thy hard-won treasures hold,
Nor dream that when life's hour is past
  Virtue alone is gold.

Dig, tott'ring fool, for Mammon's ore,
  Dig hourly, night and day,
Then die, and be for ever poor,
  For ever. Ha ! ha ! ha !

MARY'S DREAM.

PEACE, peace, for she slumbers at last,
   Poor Mary, the silent and meek,
Her season of sorrow is past,
   And leaves but a tear on her cheek.

The ghosts of her happiest years
   Come back from eternity's tomb,
Their sunshine has dried up her tears,
   For the earth is all beauty and bloom.

The home of her childhood is seen,
   That refuge most holy, most fair,
She hears merry voices within,
   Her brothers and sisters are there.

The mother is sate in the nook,
   Her children surrounding the hearth,
And often she closes her book
   To join in their innocent mirth.

But one that is dearer than these
   At eventide comes to the stile,
Youth, beauty, and goodness are his,
   That maiden how blest in his smile!

Dear moment of joy and of pride,
  He is led to that beautiful throng,
The dreamer sits down at his side,
  And voices are mingling in song.

The music hath broken the spell,
  The vision hath melted in air,
The mother that loved them so well
  Is gone from the tenantless chair.

Her brothers are far o'er the wave,
  Her sisters are scattered and wed,
Her lover—the gentle, the brave—
  Oh! where, where is he?—with the dead.

The dwelling is silent and lone,
  The dream was deceitful and vain,
The home of her childhood is gone,
  Poor Mary is weeping again.

THE LOCOMOTIVE.

THE neigh of the dragon, a terrible cry,
   Wild, piercing, and shrill, has gone up to the sky;
He pants for the start, and he snorts in his ire,
His life-blood is boiling, his heart is on fire.
His might, how terrific, how regal his train,
A comet in harness he shoots o'er the plain!
Tho' wingless, he leaves even the eagle behind,
He is strong as the torrent, as swift as the wind.
Ah! ah! gallant charger, thou flee'st at the sight,
But how slow is thy swiftness, how feeble thy might.
A moment behold him, his riders a host!
A moment, and lo! in the haze he is lost;
Afar rolls his thunder, and rises afar
The breath of his nostrils a cloud in the air,
He flies o'er a path by our fathers untrod,
A highway of wonders, the work of a God.

O man, O my brother, how stubborn thy will,
How dauntless thy courage, how godlike thy skill;
The earth, with her elements, yields to the brave,
The fire is a bondsman, the vapour a slave.
The vales are uplifted, the mountains are riven,
And the way of the dragon is shining and even.
Let us gaze and admire, and declare, if we can,
How mighty the God that created the man!

Thrice blessed the hour in which man shall confess
That pomp, art, and knowledge are powerless to bless;
Thrice blessed the day which this truth shall unfold,
That goodness is greatness, that virtue is gold;
Then man shall resemble the spirits above,
And science herself be the handmaid of love.

THE MARINERS' CHURCH.

BANKS of the Mersey! afar and on high,
   Masts like a pine forest crowding the sky,
Clouds on the water, and clouds on the shore,
This way and that way a rush and a roar;
Steamboat and omnibus each with its load
Churning the billow or shaking the road.
Crowds, like dead leaves by the whirlwind uplifted,
Hitherward, thitherward, hurried and drifted,
Hubbub and tumult for ever and ever,
Dust on the highway and foam on the river.
Pleasure boats start to the sound of the fife,
Friends of dear friends take their last look in life,
Labourer's sweat-drop and emigrant's tear
Fall down together and darken the pier;
Harlots in satin, with graces untold,
Offer you friendship, love, all things for gold;
Harlots in tatters, too, smelling of gin,
Wrecked long ago on the breakers of sin;
Merchant, whose warehouse is half of a street,
Passing poor Lazarus crouched at his feet;
Ladies and dandies, perfuming the air,
Troops of rank sweaters all heated and bare,
Numbers unnumbered, and mixed with the throngs
Men of all nations and kindreds and tongues,
Spot on the world's deck where pass in review

N

Types of the races that make up her crew,
Messmates that still, thro' Time's watches employed,
Man the great air-ship that sails thro' the void.
Thro' the dense multitudes, handsome and brave,
Moved a stout sailor boy, handsome and brave,
Dealing out freely the jest or the curse,
Joy in his countenance, gold in his purse;
Riot-wild revels and brawls in his plans,
Daring the sea's wrath and laughing at man's;
Onward he goes till a sound in his ears
Startles his soul and he burst into tears.
Suddenly, softly steal forth into air
Words of thanksgiving, repentance, and prayer;
Lo! near his feet, like a dove on her perch,
Sits on the water the Mariners' Church;
There some poor seamen, each finding a brother,
Sing of Christ Jesus, the God of his mother,
Sing to the words that in life's early years,
Lips, silent now, sweetly breathed in his ears.
Enters the prodigal, leaving without
Laughter and uproar, the curse and the shout;
Enters, and humbled, and melted, and shaken,
Turns to the Father, forgotten, forsaken;
Hearing not, heeding not, what men are saying,
Down on his knees he is weeping and praying,
Weeping and praying, while lovingly o'er him
Hovers an angel—the mother that bore him—
She whose delight was to shield and caress him,
She whose last word was a whispered "God bless him!"
Home of the homeless, one found without search,
Blessings rain on thee, O Mariners' Church!

OH! THE FLOWERS THAT ADORNED.

OH! the flowers that adorned and the sunbeams that
    lighted
The paths of our childhood are faded and cold,
And if Hope shed a beam on the spirit benighted,
    We weep to think Hope cannot cheat as of old.

How fair from the hill-top, in youth's happy morning,
    Life's journey appears to the young and the brave,
When dewdrops and blossoms, the briars adorning,
    Make pleasant the pathway that leads to the grave.

But in autumn we stand 'mid the harvests we planted,
    Unripe, yet all blasted and withered they seem,
And startled, at last we awake disenchanted,
    To know and to feel that our life is a dream.

Yet, in spite of the sadness that steals o'er the spirit,
    The thorns on the ground, and the tempests above,
Thy voice comes, dear Annie, oh, long may I hear it,
    To tell me that all is unreal but love.

FELO DE SE.

DISEASE and sorrow and care
    Had whitened his falling hair,
And hollowed out caves for his ghostly eyes;
    He slept not, he ate no food,
    A heavy and silent mood
Had sealed up the lips that knew only sighs.

    Once only he named some grief,
    Some wound beyond all relief;
Yet solace he sought not of wife or son,
    But moodily, hand on heart,
    He moaned and he walked apart,
And the thought that was in him he told to none.

    But often at dead of night
    He started in strange affright,
And turned to the ceiling his ghastly face;
    While his eye, like a lamp of fire,
    Seemed to follow in fear and ire
Some devil that moved in the throbbing space.

    Pain, pain, and a sleepless care,
    Pain, pain, and a mad despair,
Thus evermore haunted him night and day,
    Till, weary and sick of life,
    He snatched up the fatal knife
When no one was near him his hand to stay.

Some gazed on his corpse in fear,
Some over him dropt a tear,
And some of his deed made a foolish jest;
But he lay like a slave outworn,
Whose burden, too long upborne,
Had crushed out his life ere he reached his rest.

On his forehead, broad and bare,
The locks of his shining hair
Lay wild as the froth of the storm-toss'd deep;
But over his visage stole
The calm of a weary soul,
That had leaned on Mercy and fallen asleep.

Yet noble in soul was he,
And manly as man could be,
And honest and straight was the path he trod.
We ask, but none answer,—why
A nobleman so should die?
Thou knowest, thou knowest alone, O God!

ON THE DEATH OF A YOUNG LADY.

EAR and eye grew weary, weary,
    Weary even of song and light,
Weary, weary, oh ! how weary,
    Days and nights of pain and blight ;
Sweet to her the dreamless slumber,
    Welcome th' eternal night.

Bathed with tears, with blessings laden,
    Pillowed on a faithful breast,
Slowly, slowly, like the day-god,
    Sank she to her solemn rest,
While a sadness o'er our spirits
    Fell like night clouds on the West.

Mournfully we gathered round her,
    Kissed the brow and clasped the hand,
For we knew the gracious Father
    Called her to the spirit land.
Hark ! amid the breathless stillness
    Faintly sounds the seraph band !

WATERLOO.

[A traveller, just returned from the field of Waterloo, reports that it is covered with the flower "Forget-me-not." The statement gave rise to the following verses, written during the reign of Napoleon III.]

YES, 'tis the field of blood and fire,
    Where the world's madmen raged and fought.
But time has veiled its crimson mire
    With the fair flower " Forget-me-not."

'Tis well that to the lovers' wreath
    Thy bloom should lend its gentle grace ;
But on this scene of pain and death,
    How strange that thou should'st find a place.

And yet methinks 'tis not so strange,
    If from the skies the good and just,
Now purged from sin and safe from change,
    Can gaze on this once kindred dust.

Some spirit, filled with soft regret,
    Might fitly seek this tainted spot,
And here, where sin and suffering met,
    Plant the sweet flower " Forget-me-not."

Sad for Philistia's cruel lords,
    When, blinded by remorseless hate,
The Celtic Samson snapt his cords
    And grasped the pillars of their state.

But banded kings may now behold
    How strong a single nation's will!
Vain, vain the waste of blood and gold,
    For France hath her Napoleon still.

This tiny flower to great ones brings
    A wisdom that they never sought,
And whispers in the ears of kings,
    " Forget me not, forget me not."

When crowns shall lie within thy palm,
    To guard or crush them as thou wilt,
O son of toil, be wisely calm,
    And keep thy soul from regal guilt.

Should pride or envy bid thee, too,
    Seek the vain ends that despots sought,
For thee the soil of Waterloo
    Puts forth the flower " Forget-me-not."

Uplift thy shield above the poor,
    Be thine the power that loves and saves,
And let thy brethren nevermore
    Leave happy homes for bloody graves.

LINES WRITTEN AFTER SEEING THE CRYSTAL PALACE.

IT rose, a pile of wondrous grace,
   Where men of every clime and race
Stood hand in hand and face to face—
   The bard and prophet's dream!
Rome, Athens, Egypt, Babylon,
See here your noblest, best, outdone,
For still all glorious in the sun
   The crystal arches gleam!

A fane, where labour deified
Above all regal pomp and pride,
To all her living millions cried
   "The Age of Hope is come."
Wait, watch, and work, poor nameless slave,
A few more years and thou shalt have
The heritage our Father gave,
   Health, freedom, love, and home!

Let mobs and despots madly brawl,
Their rage shall work each other's fall;
But right shall triumph over all
   And worth endure for aye!

Rule like a king thy own wild heart,
Let fear, hate, envy, thence depart;
Fiends from the angel's visage start,
   As darkness flies the day.

The good, the brave, of every land,
Ennobled by the despot's brand,
Let England help with ready hand,
   The sea her sole ally.
The rocky coast and wrathful wave,
Isles full of people, strong and brave,
Without a tyrant or a slave,
   The banded world defy!

The age chivalric is *not* gone,
The world now sees there yet is one
On whose dear face the light hath shone
   Of men and angels' smiles.
Then fill the cup with rosiest wine,
Tho' reigning by no Right Divine,
Our hearts, swords, purses, yet are thine,
   Fair Ladye of the Isles.

PAINTING.

HOW beautiful is she
  Whose joy-illumined eyes
Range o'er the earth and sea,
Or seek the gorgeous landscapes of the skies,
Where, poured from golden mountains, many a stream,
  Shining like crystal, rolls
  Thro' sunniest vales, that seem
  Meet homes for blessèd souls.

Dear is the earth's green face,
  Wood, water, plain, and hill,
For her the bloom and grace
That lighted Eden rest on Nature still;
Nor do her eyes, in their wide wanderings,
  On grandeurs only dwell,
  But turn to tiniest things—
  Leaf, insect, flower, and shell.

Cloud, tempest, ocean froth,
  And hail and lightning please,
And wondrous man, in wrath
More terrible, more big with death than these.
She out of chaos bade th' Apollo come
  In naked majesty,
  That mortals, stricken dumb,
  Might feel a God was nigh.

She thro' the solemn night,
    Unblest with faintest beams,
With images of light
And beauty crowds the painter's glorious dreams—
The home of childhood, cottage, barn, and fold,
    With richest hues o'erspread,
    Where linger, as of old,
    The unforgotten dead.

Strange lands, strange peoples swim
    Before his dreamy eyes,
And visions vast and dim
Swell his young heart with wildest ecstasies;
Or while he gazes on some humble home,
    And looks on human woe,
    Tears even in slumber come,
    With sad and silent flow.

Near the far polar sky,
    Where icebergs huge, like skiffs,
On the still waters lie,
He sees the reindeer on the frozen cliffs;
Where, to the far horizon, desert sands
    Stretch, bare and hot and white,
    Near his dead camel stands
    The black-eyed Ishmaelite.

Lo! from the open grave
    Earth's noblest sons uprise,
The good, the great, the brave
Come forth to stand for ever in our eyes,
And when th' embodied dream at length is seen,
    Men in deep thought depart,
    And joy to feel within
    A softer, kindlier heart.

MOURNFUL THOUGHTS.

PURE is the stream, and pure the skies;
  The fields with joyous music ring,
And gardens load the zephyr's wing
With odours stolen from Paradise.

There, in the warm and sunny dell,
  They stand, with oaks o'er-arched above,
  Blest homes, where youthful human love
Thro' years eternal fain would dwell.

O Nature, glorious hypocrite !
  How lovely, yet how false thou art;
  Can angel lips the skill impart
To read thee and to read aright ?

A serpent coiled in flowers of spring,
  A syren that above the tides
  Shows the soft breasts of love, but hides
The scaly volumes and the sting.

From leaf, from dewdrop, flower, and sod,
  From every blade we chance to stir,
  The spoiler and the murderer
Force cries into the ears of God.

Fair seem the fields, yet on them all,
   Thro' the world's long, long weary years,
   Great drops of human sweat and tears
For ever and for ever fall.

Alas! that knowledge should destroy
   The world on which our boyhood smiled,
   That glorious world whose beauty filled
Our eyes with tears of thankful joy.

Lord, save our faith from wreck and shock,
   Amid these perils of the night;
   Let the blind eyes behold the light,
The foot, fast sinking, feel the rock.

THE POOR MAN'S RICHES.

A mean estate, a fameless name,
　　The scorn or pity of the proud,
A mind unlettered, and a frame
　　By hardest labour bowed.

All these are mine, butnot to me
　　Is life one long and vain regret,
Love, nature, music, poesy,
　　Bring joy and solace yet.

I have one daughter, young and dear,
　　And thro' the windows of her eyes
My soul, in moments sad and drear,
　　Looks into Paradise.

Fresh as the morn and soft as even,
　　And stainless is she as the dove,
Her forehead like the plains of heaven,
　　Lit with the light of love.

No painted dreams, a world's delight,
　　Your eyes within my dwelling scan,
Glimpses of Eden ere the blight
　　Had fallen on earth and man.

But from my little porch are seen
    Broad meadows and plantations fair,
Afar, the river's dancing sheen,
    And moorlands dark and bare.

And mountains lift their hoary scalps
    Up to the skies' serenest blue,
For cloud-laud has sublimer Alps
    Than any earth can show.

No voice, by patient art refined,
    Outpours for me its moving trills,
My minstrels are the harping wind,
    The ever-singing rills.

I watch the skylark as it drops,
    I listen to the linnet's call,
The starling on the chimney tops,
    The stone-chat on the wall.

Thee too, old fiddle, oft thy strings
    Rejoice, or triumph, or complain,
A needful balm thy music brings,
    For weariness or pain.

And oft some master's wizard hand
    Draws out with touches exquisite
The raptures of a seraph band,
    Or wailings from the pit.

The bard, too, soothes my grief to rest,
    His lofty themes my soul sustain,
His task how noble and how blest,
    When truth inspires the strain.

Thrice crowned is he who, scorning death,
  Sings on tho' hidden in the tomb,
And charms with unabated breath
  The ages as they come.

For the gross things we feel and see
  Let base ones wrestle—they are nought;
Mine be the world of poesy,
  The fairyland of thought.

I envy not the proud and great,
  Contented in my lone retreat,
Nor would I change this low estate
  For grandeur and a street.

THE SONG OF THE ENGLISH EMIGRANT.

OUR buried fathers rise again,
    We feel them stir in heart and vein,
Toil suits the children of the Dane,
    The Norseman woos the deep.
What tho' our task be hard and long,
Our hearts are brave, our arms are strong,
So to the sound of hopeful song
    Spread wing, thou gallant ship.

When, neath the stirless, breathless noon,
The slime creeps o'er the still lagoon,
And nature sinks as in a swoon,
    Ill bodes the sullen rest ;
We go where healthful breezes blow,
Where purer waters ebb and flow,
Weak eaglets, when the strong ones go,
    Will find a roomier nest.

We go, lest want should wed with guilt,
And swords be reddened to the hilt,
And all things that our fathers built,
    In storm and earthquake fall.
The poisoned air, the narrow space,
The rush and fight for gold and place,
Will grind to dust a noble race,
    And end in death to all.

Old scenes, old friends, tho' far we roam,
Our playmates and our early home,—
The graveyard and the mother's tomb,
　Dear to our hearts shall be.
But lo! our fathers rise again,
We feel them stir in heart and vein,
To us—the Norseman and the Dane
　Cry out, "The sea! the sea!"

THE REFORMERS' SONG.

This poetic essay was the first to appear in print, Aug. 10th, 1837.

ON, on, Reformers, ye that hold
    Britannia's freedom dear,
On, on, and high on every height
    Your glorious standard rear;
On, till the light of heaven-born truth
    Shall gild our Senate's brow,
And faction at its slightest frown
    Be brought for ever low;
On, till the plaint of want and woe
    Throughout our land be hushed,
Till home-born foes be changed to friends,
    And foes abroad be crushed;
On, on, till Learning, keen-eyed maid,
    Fair Freedom's darling child,
Make every sweating hind a sage,
    And every savage mild;
On, on, till Labour learn to smile,
    Till Right no more be rare,
Till Justice, 'gainst Oppression's might,
    Will hear the widow's prayer;
On, on, till Albion's lofty ships
    Again shall crowd the main,

Till peace and commerce o'er our isle
   Eternally shall reign,
Till patriot fire and social love
   Thro' all our ranks prevail,
And Briton thus to Briton cries,
   " Hail! friend and brother, hail ! "
On, on, while there exists a heart
   With love of freedom warmed,
On till the conquering Yellow Flag
   Wave o'er a world reformed.

A WARNING VOICE.

WHEN I was young, a fearful time it was my fate to
    know—
A time of tumult and alarm, of dearth and public woe;
Blight, plague, and poison seemed to hang between the
    earth and sky,
The smitten ploughman left his team and tottered home to
    die;
And while a prating Science filled our ears with learned talk,
The bullock perished in the stall, the grain upon the stalk.
Our ways were full of starving men—for mart and mill were
    dumb,
And a vague, unshapen, brooding fear had stilled the city's
    hum;
The rich man, passing through the crowd, grew ashen with
    dismay,
For poor men looked upon the rich as panthers on their prey.
As, sad of heart and slow of foot, along the streets I passed,
My ears and heart were startled with a trumpet's sudden
    blast,
And, turning round, my eyes beheld within the open square
A stranger, wild in act and mien, with ragged beard and
    hair.
His garb was worn and travel-stained, his features all
    aglow,
Seeming like one that came in haste and was in haste to go;

Poor, hollow-eyed, and gaunt was he, yet full of pride and
 ire,
His keen grey eyeballs flashing with a seer or madman's fire.
There, in the spacious market place, the pilgrim took his
 stand,
And faced the crowd with steadfast gaze and lean uplifted
 hand ;
His trumpet to his bearded lips the stranger raised again,
And thrice he launched upon the wind a weird and mourn-
 ful strain :—
"That is the knell of things that are," saith he, "a sound
 that brings
Wailing to palaces and shakes the thrones of wicked kings;
The priests and rulers of the earth, with all that own their
 sway,
By famine, sword, and pestilence shall all be swept away ;
Guilty before the court in heaven earth's warring kingdoms
 stand,
The dreadful sentence has gone forth—the judgment is at
 hand.
Wail ! wail, ye cruel kings ! that o'er the innocent and
 weak
So long have raised the lion's paw or eagle's gory beak.
And wail, ye lying priests, that saw without rebuke or frown
God's children bound in slavish chains—in battles trodden
 down.
Ye take the widow's only son from honest toils away,
And fill his heart with rage and hate, and teach him how to
 slay ;
Ye claim the lives of men and say ye reign by right divine,
Yet waste your days in vain pursuits—in harlotry and wine.
Dead nations, like accusing ghosts rise up, that for your pride
Rained sweat-drops on the sodden ground, or rolled in blood
 and died.

For twice two thousand years this mortal human agony
Has sent up to the patient heavens its long and piteous cry;
The signs and wonders in the clouds forebode the hour that
    brings
Down to the earth the Lord of lords, the mighty King of
    kings.
Woe to the great ones of the earth that trust to spear and
    bow,
An arrow from the widow's son shall lay the mightiest low;
The soldier, like a maddened steed, shall snap his brittle
    chain,
And by the sword that power supplied shall godless power
    be slain.
The demons of the nether pit shall execute his wrath,
And hell, unloosed, lay waste the world and clear the Con-
    queror's path,
All tyrannies that bind the soul shall then be overthrown,
While high above the shattered thrones the Lord shall set
    His own.
Then shall a remnant bow the knee, while men and angels
    sing,
' Jesus, the Slain, the Crucified, of heaven and earth is
    King.'
And wheresoe'er the sunlight falls, the evil beast shall cease,
And men shall see the reign of love, of righteousness and
    peace.
Lord, let the glory of Thy throne the universe o'erspan,
For power and love unite in Thee, O Son of God and Man."
Then on his own mysterious way the wild-eyed pilgrim went,
And, turning thrice, cried out aloud, "Repent! Repent!
    Repent!"

OUR FATHER'S HOME.

HOW eloquent the tongueless things
    That stand around our father's home,
Each stone, a silent wizard, brings
    The past as from a tomb.

Dear be the house where round the fire
    Fair loving faces were arrayed,
Where brother, sister, mother, sire,
    Joyed, sorrowed, wept, and prayed.

Dear be the home, tho' strangers claim
    The roof that screened our father's head,
And none, alas ! remain to name
    The absent or the dead.

Most dear, most holy, for even yet
    Hearth, meadow, garden, tree, and stone
Forbid the living to forget
    The dear ones that are gone.

Hallowed and loved for ever be
    That old abode of human love,
'Tis heaven to dream that we may see
    A home like that above.

THE AGE OF POESY IS GONE.

NAME, gold, and power alone can bless,
   So mortals look not heavenward now,
But guideless, godless, fatherless,
   Bend to the base earth heart and brow.

This world is but a timepiece, formed
   To wear away its springs and stop,
So hearts grow cold and dead, unwarmed,
   Unvivified by Faith and Hope.

Tho' the Creator's living laws
   All things in heaven and earth control,
God, or God's work, no longer draws
   Awe, love, or wonder from the soul.

Hearts, yearning for a father's love,
   Shed orphans' tears and feel alone,
Mammon hath quenched the lights above—
   The Age of Poesy is gone.

And is it so? Speak, sons of thought,
   Who, looking ever to the skies,
Have, in the soul's deep stillness, caught
   Heaven's loftiest, holiest harmonies.

Man cannot live unsoothed by song,
  Sick of this world's low cares and pain,
The fainting soul will turn, ere long,
  To hear the minstrel's harp again.

THE BROKEN LYRE.

VAINLY God's voice is heard
　　For ever day and night,
Whose wakened echoes stirred
All human hearts with wonder and delight.
Men look not upward in this evil day,
　　But all to Mammon given,
　　The spirit weds the clay,
　　And earth is loosed from heaven.

There, on the sterile heath
　　Poor mortals pining sit,
Or grope and delve beneath
The smoke and darkness of the infernal pit;
World-wisdom lights them, and its lying glare
　　Their hearts have learned to love,
　　So the clear holy star
　　Shines vainly from above.

So, o'er the Broken Lyre,
　　Dashed down in wrath and tears,
She wept, whose eye of fire
Once lit all eyes with radiance caught from hers;
Wept in her bitterness of soul to see
　　Men and good angels part,
　　And faith, love, Deity,
　　Die in the human heart.

Now, e'er she seeks the skies
From yon far moonlit steep,
She thro' her seraph's eyes
Looks down on Nature in her solemn sleep.
Her eyes are like the day-god's parting beams,
Her face, all cloud-beclad,
Like a June sunset seems,
Most glorious, yet most sad.

And from their homes above,
The everlasting spheres,
In sorrow and in love,
Look down thro' eyes that glisten as with tears;
And mournfully the wand'ring night-wind sigheth
O'er mountains bare and lone,
And the deep sea replieth
With deeper, sadder moan.

THE SUNSET.

SADLY o'er the purple mountain
  Fades the crimson light,
Sadly o'er the still creation
  Comes the solemn night ;
Stirless in the awful twilight
  Stands the ruined pile,
Faintly yet the ivied turrets
  Catch the sun's last smile.

Darkly 'gainst the pale horizon
  Pine trees lift the head,
Motionless they stand, like mourners
  Round a dying bed.
Hark! the redbreast from yon elm tree,
  Thro' the distance dim,
Gazing on the dying day-god
  Sings the funeral hymn.

Lo! the spectral moon uprising
  Glides o'er land and main,
Like the ghost of the departed
  Walking forth again ;
Ask ye why the solemn sunset
  Causeth tears to come ?
'Tis because it saith, O mortal,
  Thou, too, hast a tomb.

Ah ! how sadly o'er the spirit
   Spirit shadows fall,
Telling of a night eternal
   Dark with shroud and pall.
Life but seems a dream-creation,
   Vain its joys, hopes, fears,
So the heart's unuttered sadness
   Overflows in tears.

THE REDBREAST.

ON the yellow spray
    He, like the white-haired prophet,
        sits alone,
A mourner among ruins, thro' the day
    Making melodious moan.

    While the wintry rime
Falls on his wings, the lone, last minstrel pours
Wild fitful farewells to the sunny time,
    Low requiems o'er the flowers.

    Or, on lowly sheds
Thou sittest, voiceless with unmeasured woe,
While o'er the cold dead summer, winter spreads
    A winding sheet of snow.

    Give thy sorrow scope,
Or from the frozen bough or withered leaf
Speak soothingly, in whispers such as Hope
    Breathes in the ears of Grief.

    Sing the coming hours,
The warm, glad sheen of living spring foretell,
When happy children, laden with bright flowers,
    Return from brook and dell.

So, thro' life's dull years,
The soul's unlovely winter, I from thee
May draw some solace, and thro' mists and tears
Gaze on the bright *to be*.

THE IRISH EMIGRANT.

HE stands beside his father's grave,
   Dumb, pale, and motionless as one
From whom strength, hope, and life had gone ;
To-morrow, and the ocean wave
Will roll between that sire and son ;
To-morrow !—Oh, that bursting heart !
The sleeper and the mourner part.

'Tis not the sigh, 'tis not the tear,
That tells the voiceless sorrow there—
That stony gaze alone can speak
For hearts that would but cannot break.
The dreams that mocked his hopes are past,
All sunshine from his sky is gone,
Famine and grief have chased at last
All wishes from that breast but one—
The one wish that the wretched have,
The wish, the hunger for the grave.
He prays. That worn and abject man
Kneels o'er the form beneath him laid,
And helplessness cries out for aid
More earnestly than language can ;
And poor and wretched tho' he be—
A thing that, in its power and pride,
A thankless world has cast aside—

Yet not in vain that bended knee,
That mute but pleading agony.
Alone, self-banished, he shall roam
From all he loves to other lands,
Where the hard toil of honest hands
Is worth a morsel and a home ;
Or, haply, he may be even there
A beggar still, as he is here.
The friendly clasp, the kindly word,
May never more be felt or heard,
But there, amid a wasting strife,
With cold, home-sickness, penury,
He may unknown, unheeded, die
The long death of a loveless life.

Ah ! why has grandeur from him torn
His portion of the common soil—
Nay, even forbid, with bitter scorn,
This outcast of the land to toil,
When all things else of heaven receive
The right to labour and to live ?

THE ORPHAN.

IT seemed most pitiful that one
  So gentle and so innocent
Should, ere the daylight dawned, be sent
To walk the wastes of life alone.
Too low to ope the door when shut,
It was no wonder he should fail
To make the dull world hear his wail.
Poor outcast nestling! he was but
The plaything of the savage wind,
And, wond'ring at a wrath so blind,
Full soon his failing wings he furled.
What though he cried for help, and prayed
More earnestly as strength decayed,
This prating, bustling, busy world,
Driven onward by its sordid cares,
Stopped not to listen to his prayers;
So he grew weaker day by day,
And when the summer months were passed,
He, bowed and broken by the blast,
In a poor widow's cottage lay.
Sick was the head and worn the frame,
And soul and body, sore opprest,
Sighed for the grave's enduring rest,
And eyes, grown weary of the light,
Longed for the everlasting night;
So down from heaven at last there came

A swift and smiling messenger,
Who, all unheard and unbeheld,
Save by the sick and waiting child,
Breathed a soft whisper in his ear,
I know not what the angel said,
But when a brief and joyous light
Had o'er the visage, worn and white,
Passed like a sunbeam—he was dead.

HYMN TO POVERTY.

HAIL! mother of immortal men,
   Hail! nurse of children, half divine;
The heroes of the sword and pen,
   The demi-gods of earth, are thine.

How vain the boast of regal tongues,
   The lightning of the imperial glance,
When Toil, from mighty heart and lungs,
   Sent up the war-cry, "Vive la France."

On many a field the record stands
   Of battles fearful hard and hot,
Where peasant leaders, peasant bands,
   The chivalry of Europe smote.

Say, Nature, hath our God decreed
   To veil thee from the poor man's eyes?
May none, save great ones, hope to read
   Thy unimagined mysteries?

Lo! names unknown to titled pride
   The noblest births of mind display;
The steamer rushing through the tide,
   The dragon of the iron way.

Half-buried in the down of case,
　High bards have sung the choir among,
And marble halls and palaces
　Have echoed with undying song.

But nations hushed and tearful stand
　As, prompted by divinest fire,
A ploughboy's gnarled and rugged hand,
　With wizard touches, stirs the lyre.

We deem not great or noble now
　Whom kings have made so with a word—
Abashed, let man-made greatness bow
　Before the anointed of the Lord.

MUSIC.

A MAID, whose home is heaven,
    Sate in the crimson light
Which at the solemn even
Is wont to linger on the mountain's height;
  All hushed, as tho' no more to wake and weep,
    The world in dreamless lull
    Lay, like a babe asleep,
      Most still, most beautiful.

Closed were the soft blue eyes,
    Tho' ocean, air, and earth,
And the awaking skies,
Seemed glorious as the Eden of her birth;
  At last, a wailing night wind, like a soul,
    Swept o'er the fluttering wood,
    And, fainting, dying, stole
      Up to her solitude.

A joy unutterable
    The starting list'ner filled,
As slowly rose and fell
The ghostly music—fitful, mournful, wild;
  They come like voices to her charmèd ear,
    Those wand'ring sounds that roam,
    Like spirits thro' the air,
      And seek but find no home.

She heard the bee that stirred
 The noontide, hushed and hot,
The brook, the cheery bird,
And dewdrop, tinkling in the haunted grot;
 Nor less she loved to hearken to the dash
  Of the wind-beaten main,
 Or sudden thunder crash,
  Rending the heavens in twain.

And sounds of wrath and power
 Pleased, tho' they paled her cheek—
The lion's midnight roar,
Or the red battle's crash and shout and shriek;
 Nor turned she from those deeper, sadder tones,
  Uttered alone, apart,
 The wailings and the groans
  Wrung from the human heart.

At last, her earnest eyes,
 Lit with an inward fire,
Looked upward to the skies
Whence her mute prayer drew down a seraph's
 lyre,
 Then holiest strains, divinest melodies,
  To the wide air were flung,
 And mortals bowed their knees
  When music found a tongue.

MY GRONFATHUR'S GRAVE.

NUT a puff stirred a leaf o' them grand owd trees,
   'At owershaddad the grahnd ov ahr village church,
As I gloared wi' full een on a gerse-grown heap,
  Under t'shade of a knotted an' time-worn birch.

T''owd tree, like a priest in his hoaly robes,
   Stude solemn an' grey anent t'western dlow,
An' liftin' its arms into t'silent air,
   Seemed to pray for t'poar fellah 'at slept below.

T'lois at hand a fine marble wor placed aboon t'squire,
   Thau he stale fro' his tenants ther hard-won breead,
For it's tyrants, 'at grunds uz wi' pahr an' brass,
   'At we honour an' worship alive ur decad.

Bud ye'll fynd nauther tablet, nur name, nur date,
   Ovver t'spot wheer my gronfathur sleeps i' t'dark,
For this world tak's na gaum ov a sweeatin' slave
   'At can nobbud due useful an' honist wark.

Nut a letter he knew ov his a b c's,
   Nut a pothuke his fingurs could frame ta mak',
So they made ov a brother a harnessed beast,
   'An a beast's heavy burden oppressed his back.

Fro' five ov a mornin' to nine at neet
   He slaved for a livin' for forty year,
An' all t'plessur 'at sweetened that bitter life
   Wor a Sunday stretch an' a pint o' beer.

Then they tuke him away fro' his flail an' plew,
   An' they streytened him intuv a sowjer lad,
For his reulers, althan they could read an' write,
   Hed been lakin' a lifetime at " Hell run mad."

An' if ivver, when trodden reyt dahn i' t'muck,
   His heart in a whisper hed said, " Rebel,"
His tyrants hed cheyns for body an' sowl—
   I' this life a dungeon, i' t'next a hell.

Hay, dear ! hah we suffered thru pride an' greed,
   When t'country wor governed by nowblemen ;
Them lords 'at says t'poar isn't fit to reul,
   Sud lewk ovver t'webs they've wovven thersen.

Poor grondad, I wish tha wor here to see
   Hah bravely we've battled wi' pahr an' brass,
Fur t'day draws near when a king munnot craw
   Ovver t'ignarant, impidant workin' class.

When I think o' t'long ahrs an' o' t'slavish wark
   'At browt tha so sooin tuv a naamless tomb,
My courage revives, an' my arm an' neiv
   Gets strung up an' doubled for t'feyt to come.

VARRY FINE FOWK.

HIP Hurrah! Hip Hurrah! whot a hullabaloo!
    I sud think 'at thear nivver wor sich an a doo.
Lukin' this way ur that, thear wor women by t'score,
Awther scramlin' fur t'window ur makin' to t'doar.
T''little barns ran wi' t'news ovver t'village like hares;
Hah they scuttard dahn ginnels an' scamper'd up stairs!
Then they pearkt like young sparrows on t'capestuns
     o' t'wall,
Singin' " T''fine fowk is comin' to Tumaldahn Hall! "
T''owd place wor i' bits, an' all t'gardins a waste,
Bud some varry fine fowk com ta rent it at t'last.
As they rade up to t'gates in a carriage an' pair
Ahr village wor ommost as threng as a fair;
Whot wi' silks an' wi' satins, an' ribbons an' flahrs,
Them gentle-fowk glittered like newly-snuffed stars;
T''owd chap lewkt a general ur summat o' t'soart,
An' his dowters like ladies connected wi' t'court;
Wer een, I can tell ya, wor dazzled wi' t'shine,
Coach, coachman, an' harniss an' all wor so fine.

Theas fearful fine bodies at Tumaldahn Hall
Made t'poar i' ther neighbourhood feel varry small,
For t'best o' whativver wer land could produce
Hed ta go to t'big hahse fur them gentle-fowk's use.
Thear wor nowt i' this kingdom ta gooid ur ta dear
Fur a man at hed noab'dy knew hah mich i' t'year.

If ya wautud fresh eggs ye cud hev um no moar,
Offer tuppence a-piece an' they'd shew ya to t'doar;
Reddy brass wodn't buy um, nut even for t'sick,
For they went up to t'Hall at three-awpence on t'tick.
Theas varry fine fowk, mun, wor varry mich sowt,—
Bless yer sowl, t'wor a plezzer to sarve um fur nowt.

Once I went dahn to t'butcher I'd knawn all my life,
An' touched a prime joint wi' t'tip end ov his knife ;
" What's t'price o' this here, lad, it seems varry good? "
" Ay—that's bahn up to t'Hall, for Sir Evverton Hood ;
Sin' a carriage an' pair began stoppin' at t'doar,
My meyt's goan off better nor ivver before.
I'd be reared wi' such like if I'd nobbud a few,
Thear's nowt like a shew, lad, thear's nowt like a shew."
" Aw ! thinks ta," I said, " then ta mak' a display ;
I sal stop, wi' t'owd mule, when I'm cartin' some hay."
Then I went into t'main street, an' lewkin' abaht,
I spied summat tasty, an' ventured ta shaht,
" Just weigh ma that cod-heead 'at's liggin' on t'stall ! "
" Tha'rt to lat', lad, that cod-heead is bahn up to t'Hall."
" Well, I can't dew wi' fish when it's young, dus ta see,
If tha's hearin's a month owd, I'll tak' two ur three."
Then owd Cobb, wi' an oath, made a grab at his knife,
So I slipt threw a ginnil, an' cut fur my life.
Then I saw a gurt board shahtin' aht i' big type,
" Penny ducks an' black puddin', sheep trotters an' tripe.'"
" Aw, my hearty," I said, as I glored ovver t'stall,
I fun summat at last 'at's noan bahn up to t'Hall."
Soa I pooled aht my purse, an' I ate—I knawn't what—
Bud I relished it rarely, an' dahn'd a gooid lot.
When ye're eytin' owd hen if ya knawn't what it is,
Ye can fancy it's turkey, ur owt 'at ya please,
T'owd gen'ral hisseln, up at Tumaldahn Hall,

Nivver feastud so weel at a party ur ball,
Nur his delicate dowters, 'at sigh'd aht ther begs
Wi' t'fattest o' pullets an' t'freshest o' eggs.
My desart wor sarved up at yond shant o' Jack Heys,
'Twor a bottle o' pop an' a saucer o' peys.
A time com' at last, when all t'tradesmen abaht
Hed used up ther chalk an' wur lewkin' fur t'claht.
Bud Sir Evverton Hood put um off wi' a smile,
Touched um all wi' a fether fair sodden wi' oil,
Spak o' land i' Jimaka, ur somewheers abroad,
An' o' cargoes o' cotton an' sewgar on t'road;
Then he promised once moar ivvry promise ta keep,
An' he smoothed dahn ther brussels an' rockt um ta sleep.
Then his dowters wor ta'en wi' a short holla cough,
An' a doctor wor called on 'at ordered um off.
In a while comes a letter fro' Naples ur Rome,
Sayin' t'dowters wor deein' an' t'fathur mud come.
Soa he rade dahn ta t'station, tuke t'train in a crack,
Bud t'tradesmen can tell ya, he's nivver come back.
T'owd chap wor a scholar o' wonderful parts,
An' a—what is't they call it?—aw! Master of Arts.
Ye've seen, at wer galas i' Mannygam Park,
Them rockits an' sich, 'at goas up after dark,
All endin' i' smook, an' a bad-smellin' cowk—
Them shiners reminds me o' VARRY FINE FOWK.

HAPPY TIPPY.

I LUKE for a dlimmer whenivver it's dark,
  I whissel when t'winter wind ovver ma blaws,
Thau i' summer it's pleasant ta hearken ta t'lark,
  Yit I like a tomtit 'coss he sings when it snaws.

When I cannot get beef I tak treacle an' breead,
  An' I laugh at all boggards whativver ther shape ;
I sal nivver seek sorra nur wish mysen deead
  Wol t'sun's donn'd i' mournin' an' t'sky's 'ung wi' crape.

This world's noan a bad un ta them 'at's nut bad,
  An' wur life isn't awlus a moil an' a toil,
For at times, thau I'm forty, I feel like a lad,
  An' I lowp ovver t'gap-rail as leet as a foil.

I'm a poor workin' chap donn'd i' fushtan, ye see,
  An' I addle wi' sweeat ivvry penny I draw ;
Bud there's noabdy, I guess, at's as happy as me,
  For I'm t'ansomist fella yer een ivver saw.

I've a grand little wife i' yon cosey owd cot,
  An' a bonnier lass nivver stept aht o' door,
An' bless her, shoo'd wit ta pick me aht o' t'lot,
  Thau her sweethearts i' number wor ommost a score.

I've a lad abaht eight, thau he lewks nobbud small,
  At writin' an' cahntin' he's t'topmost o' t'list ;
He's a rare hand at plonk-taw, an' better nur all,
  He can lick ivvery scholar i' t'schooil wi' his fists.

He can play on t'tin whissel, an' sing " Hold the Fort,"
  He can bahl a streyt ball an' can hannal his bat ;
He's a topper is Jack, boath at leearnin an' spoart,
  An' he'll some day be t'member fur t'Borrough will that.

I've a darlin' i' petticoits cloise upon seven,
  An' fur bewty shoo taks after t'mother an' me ;
Mun, I feel as if really I'd getten ta heaven
  When shoo tunes up i' t'eemins atop o' my knee.

A lass wi' a sweeter voice nivver wor born,
  An i' what they call glees shoo can tak up her pairt ;
Him at plays o' t' peeanna at t'Hunter and Horn,
  Says he'll match her to sing Jenny Lind for a quairt.

Nah, if ivver a pig wor a pictur' o' luck
  It's a sue 'at ahr Margit hes getten i' t'sty ;
It's grand ta be near her an' watch her gie suck
  Ta young uns 'at breeders is lengin ta buy.

Then beside all my pigs I've a tarrier bitch,
  Shoo's a fahl un bud then in a famine shoo'l thrive,
After t'rabbits shoo'l run fur two mile at a stretch,
  An' t'rattan shoo sees hesn't a minnit ta live.

Soa wi' t'world an' its troubles I'm willin' ta feyt,
  Fur its roses is sweet thau its nettles may sting ;
I can sleep like a top, I can relish my meyt,
  An' I live wi' t'owd lass as content as a king.

I lewk for a dlimmer whenivver it's dark,
   I whissel when t'winter wind ovver me blaws,
Than it's pleasant i' summer ta hearken to t'lark,
   Yit I like a tomtit 'coss he sings when it snaws.

ALEXANDER'S SURFEIT.

A PARODY ON ALEXANDER'S FEAST.

'TWAS at an auction sale the deed was done,
    For guineas twenty-one :
Aloft in awful state
The hammer-wielder sate
    On his unstable throne :
His beery helps were placed around,
Their brows with 'kerchiefs and with plasters bound,
    So should assistant rogues be crowned.
Two lovely Broadwoods at his side
Stood, as if wanting to be tried,
In all the pomp of varnished pride.
    Flimsy, flashy, trashy pair,
      None but a knave,
      None *but* a knave,
    None but a *knave* would sell such ware.

The salesman placed on high,
    'Mid that discordant choir,
    Bade some one smite the stringed wire :
The jangling notes ascend the sky,
    And happy jokes inspire.
A curled professor, fair as Jove,
Forsook his clerkly seat above
To play the Broadwood of his love ;

He took his seat with knowing smile and nod,
And while his radiant teeth he showed,
In whispers thus his soul expressed :
" I call this thing the crown of art, the banger of the world."
The gaping crowd admire the thund'rous sound,
" A glorious instrument " they shout around.
" A glorious instrument " the vaulted roofs rebound :

    With ravished ears
    Old Alick hears ;
    His drunken nod
    The wire and wood
   For aye to him transfers.

The praise of Crochett then old Alick's daughter sung,
  Of Crochett looking ever fair and young :
  The teacher soon in triumph comes,
  Sweet the modern air he hums ;
  With more of cheek than grace
  He shows his flushing face,
Now, lady, mind your heart, he comes ! he comes !
  Crochett, looking ever young,
  Music lessons doth ordain ;
  Tho' said lessons cost a treasure,
  Music is the maiden's pleasure :
    Rich the treasure,
    Sweet the pleasure,
  Sweet is pleasure bought with pain.

  Scared with the sounds, the sire in vain
  Wished all his guineas back again,
And thrice he cursed the auctioneer, and thrice he cursed
  his men.
   The tutor saw the madness rise,
   His redd'ning cheeks, his flashing eyes,

And while he thumb to nose applied,
Changed the tune, and saved his hide.
He chose a mournful muse,
Soft pity to infuse,
He sang the prince so great and good,
By too severe a fate
Fallen, fallen, fallen, fallen,
Fallen from his charger's height,
And weltering in his blood;
Deserted in his utmost need
By those his fearless valour led,
In Caffirland exposed he lies,
With not a friend to close his eyes.
  With downcast looks the joyless father sate,
  Revolving in his altered soul
    The various tricks of trade below,
  And now and then a sigh he stole
    While gazing at his shoe.

  The music-master smiled to see
  Despair was in the next degree:
  Small cause will angry fathers move
  To take the liquors that they love.
    Softly sweet with Lydian measures,
    Soon he turned his soul to pleasures;
  Trade, he sang, is toil and trouble,
  Civic honours but a bubble,
  Buying, selling, carding, spinning,
    Meanest tricks and arts employing,
  If the gold be worth thy winning,
    Think, oh think it worth enjoying!
Port and sherry stand beside thee,
Take the drink the gods provide thee.
The street boys rent the skies with loud applause,

And raised a row, but music was the cause.
  The sire, unable to conceal his pain,
      Gazed on the pair
      Who caused his care,
    And sighed and looked, sighed and looked,
    Sighed and looked, and sighed again.
At length, with grief and wine at once oppress'd,
The father turned away and sought his rest.

    They bang the jangling wires again :
    A louder yet, and yet a louder strain
    Broke the bands of sleep asunder,
    And roused him like a rattling peal of thunder.
      Hark ! hark !   The horrid sound
        Has raised up his head,
        As awaked from the dead,
      And amazed he stares around.
" Revenge ! Revenge ! " old Alick cries.
        See his fury rise !
        See the shirt in his rear,
        How it floats on the air,
      And the sparkles that flash from his eyes !
        How long will he stand
        With the light in his hand,
Like to one of the ghosts that in battle were slain,
        And unburied remain
        Inglorious on the plain ?
        For the vengeance due
        How the old cock crew !
Behold, how he tosses the waltzes on high,
How he rages and gibbers, and stamps and nods,
And curses and swears by the underground gods !
The street boys applaud with a furious joy,
And the sire seized a poker with zeal to destroy ;

Betsy stopt the way,
To turn him from his prey,
And like another athlete floored the good old boy.

Ah! long ago,
Ere heaving bellows learned to blow,
While organs yet were mute,
Street minstrels with a noisy flute,
Or jingling lyre,
Could spoil our noonday nap and kindle fierce desire.
But sadder still at last there came
The inventor of this vocal frame;
That cursed enthusiast, from his horrid store,
Enlarged the former narrow bounds,
And added strength to horrid sounds,
With Satan's mother wit and arts unknown before.
Old Alick fain would yield his prize,
And hopes some power unknown
Will take his Broadwood to the skies,
And bring an angel down.

THE STORY OF ABEL BEN ABOO.

A PROSE POEM.

LONG ago, when a young man, I was the servant of David, the rich Jew of Aleppo. One day my master bade me load the camels with merchandise and depart for a distant city. But I said, " O my master, at this season robbers are lying in wait on the skirts of the wilderness, and the way is full of danger as a lion's mouth." Then the Jew, my master, grew angry, and looking scornfully upon me, said, "Thy mother will weep when I tell her that she hath brought forth a hare that flees from the falling leaf." When I heard that, I too grew angry and cried out, " Dog of a Jew, hold thy peace, lest I thrust thee through with my dagger. Since the day I entered thy house thy words have ever been bitter,—bitter as the juice of the aloe tree and sharper than the sword of Saladin. May thy right hand be smitten with palsy, and thy face in the day of judgment be blacker than charcoal."

The Jew, so soon as I had cursed him, waxed exceeding wroth, and spat in my face; whereupon I smote him on the forehead, so that he fell down backwards, and lay as one dead. Then a great fear came upon me, and in my heart I began to curse my Maker, seeing that he had suffered me to fall into this snare of the devil. "Oh Abel!" I cried, "to-morrow thy head will be nailed to the gate of the city, and thy carcase cast from its walls to be devoured by dogs. Henceforth who shall put his trust in God, or keep the commandment of His prophet?"

In the midst of my lamentation—blessed for evermore be the name of Allah—I saw the lips of the Jew move, and kneeling down beside him, I heard him mutter curses on his servant, whereby I knew he was not dead—only for a time stunned and disabled. Then I hearkened to a voice within me which said, "O Abel, tarry thou not to help thy master, for when he cometh to himself he will drag thee before the governor, who will cause thy feet to be beaten with rods." So I girded up my loins with intent to leave the city in haste, for I knew the governor was an unjust man, that despised the poor, and hearkened to him whose bags were full of silver. Suddenly, however, I bethought me that I had no money, so I snatched the purse from the Jew's girdle, and took therefrom ten pieces of silver, the wages due to me, and seeing that he had well nigh provoked me to slay him, I took other ten pieces also, to bear the costs of my journey. "Doubtless," said I, "when the Hebrew counteth up his coins he will blaspheme the prophet, and curse his servant; but what saith Nazim, the Arabian poet, 'The ass that treadeth upon a serpent shall be bitten on the heel.'"

When I had travelled about half a day's journey, I turned aside from the highway, saying, "Here will I abide till the night cometh."

An hour after midday, as I looked towards Aleppo, I saw a cloud of dust, then the glittering points of two spears, then two horsemen riding towards me on the wings of the tempest. When they arrived opposite my hiding place they cried out to a goatherd in the field, "Knowest thou aught of Abel, the servant of David the Jew?" "Yea," said the goatherd, "I saw him at noontide, going towards Aleppo by way of the sheep-folds." It was not I, but a man like unto me, that he had seen, driving his beasts to the city. When I saw the soldiers of the governor turn the heads of their horses, I remembered the words of a holy Dervish, "The wisdom of the wise and the ignorance of the fools work out together the purposes of God and confound the enemies of the faithful."

When the sun rose I was far from Aleppo, and changing my apparel for the garb of a shepherd, I turned my face towards Jerusalem. While I was yet a day's journey from the Holy City, I saw two men bending over another lying on the ground. As I drew near I saw that the two men were Syrian guides, and that he who lay upon the ground was from the land of the Franks. One of the guides was opening the vest of his master, while the other applied to his nostrils a small phial out of which came a piercing odour. "What aileth this stranger?" I asked. "Smitten by the sun," said one of his attendants. "Thy words," said I, "come from the mouth of a fool; seest thou not that the hands of thy master are clenched, and that there is foam upon his lips? Behold," said I, "this man is torn inwardly by a devil. Stand aside, in the name of Mohammed, Prophet of the Most Merciful, and ye shall see this fiend driven out of him." So saying, I drew from my bosom a ruby which had touched the sacred stone at Mecca, and applied it to his forehead. Instantly the hands were unclenched, the eyes were opened, and the demoniac looked around him as one that waketh up suddenly out of deep sleep. Truly the words of the Persian Sage are wise, for he saith, "The spirits of the damned are the slaves of the Most High, but the faithful are His children, and shall rule over them."

When the stranger came to himself, he asked my name, and besought me to abide with him, as the guides wished to return to their own homes. Bowing my face to the earth, I told him I was willing to become his slave, and follow him even to the shores of the Great Sea.

At eventide, when we encamped, he called me into his tent and told me that he was an Englishman who had fled from snow and frost to the sunshine of the East. "Twice, O Abel," said he, "have I been nigh unto death, but a wise physician hath told me that the warm air and delicious fruits of Asia may perchance restore me to perfect health." "Alas, my master," said I, "put no trust in the physician thou speakest of, he hath been nourished from childhood with the milk of asses, and his wisdom is but witchcraft and folly." "Say not so," said the young lord, "for my physician is a great man among the Franks, and his head contains the hoarded knowledge of a school that hath existed a hundred years." "Hath England a Jerusalem or a Damascus? Behold!" said I, "your nation is a babe of yesterday, and knows not the wisdom that hath come down to us through the ages. Here, O my master, is a ruby that shall avail thee more than all the skill in Europe. Bind it around thy neck, and neither the imps of Tophet nor the genii that bowed the knee to King Solomon will ever molest thee again." "I will even do as thou sayest," said he, and putting the string round his neck, he hid the gem in his bosom, and I saw by the smile on his lips that he felt safe and happy as one that reposes in the shadow of God.

When we arrived at Jerusalem, the city was in an uproar, for the Infidels had come from the ends of the earth to fight with one another at the grave of the man they call Jesus. Early in the morning my master called me to his side, and said, "O Abel, show me the wonders of the place." So, after we had washed our faces, and eaten bread, we went forth into the street. The soldiers of Abdul the Mighty were riding to and fro with drawn scimitars, keeping apart the hostile sects that growled at each other like the wolves of the desert. "O my lord," said I, "thou seest here one of the wonders of the city; these be the followers of him whom they call the Prince of Peace." Then I led my master to the Church of the Holy Sepulchre, saying at the door thereof, "Enter, and I will wait for thee." But the Frank said, "Abel, come thou with me, and see the wonders of the place." "Not so, my lord," said I, "a servant of the true God may not look on the pictures and images which these idolaters have set up in the land of his prophet." Afterwards I showed him the hundred places made famous by the Christians; and when I heard the monks tell of the wonders and miracles of their church, I marvelled that he should believe them, till I remembered the words of Ahmed the Sage—"He that rejects the wisdom that comes from heaven shall be filled with the falsehoods of hell."

On the following morning my master again called me to his side, saying, " Abel, to-day thou shalt show me the places held in honour by the faithful." "Behold," said I, "in all Jerusalem there is nothing to compare with the Mosque of Omar; let us go thither, and in place of the legends of lying and deceitful monks, thou shalt hear the traditions that comfort the souls of believers."

When we reached the holy place I showed him the great rock in the middle of the temple, on which Abraham was about to offer up his son Isaac. " Even the sacred books of the Christians," said I, "make mention of this stone and of the intended sacrifice. It was from this rock," said I, "that Mohammed ascended into heaven, but when the sacred stone was rising also, it was seized and held down by Gabriel." "The story is too wonderful," said my master, but when I showed him the footprints of the prophet, and the marks made by the archangel's fingers, his doubtings were rebuked, and I saw that he stood confounded.

In Jerusalem my master tarried a whole month, going hither and thither to see divers places in the neighbourhood. When he had satisfied the eye with seeing, he said, "Let us depart for Jaffa, and there take ship for Egypt." So I hired two camels for the baggage and a horse for my master.

As we journeyed towards the seaport, I saw coming from thence a train of camels laden with the merchandise of the West. In front thereof walked a Nubian, blacker than the wings of Azrael, and behind, seated on an ass, rode an accursed dog of the Hebrew race. As we passed the train I lifted up my eyes to look at the man who rode the ass, and behold! it was the Jew, David of Aleppo!

When my late master saw me, he cursed me with a loud voice in Hebrew and in Arabic, proclaiming me a robber and a murderer. Then, driving his beast close up to my side, he whispered, " Forsake thou this stranger and return with me, and when thou hast served me a year thy evil deed shall be forgiven."

" Jew," said I, " Abel the camel driver defies thee. When the Bedouin took from thee a bundle of shawls near Jericho, didst thou not blaspheme the Prophet and call upon thy God to curse his followers? Move but thy little finger against me and I will cause thy tongue to be cut out and nailed to the door of the synagogue. And why temptest thou me to forsake this stranger? Behold," said I, " my master is a king's son. His presence is grateful as the shade of the palm tree; his voice as pleasant the sound of running waters; his table fruitful in all good things as the gardens about Damascus; and his purse the pap of a she camel pouring out plenty of milk evening and morning. As for thee, thou art an infidel and the son of a witch; thy mouth is a nest of scorpions, thy table a cornfield which the locusts have forsaken, thy right hand without a gift and barer than the desert."

Having ended my speech we journeyed on, leaving the Jew behind us. Then my master, riding up to me, said " Abel, what said that Hebrew ? "

"Of a truth," said I, "his words were these, 'Forsake thou this stranger, and return with me ; ' " but I told him not the rest, for Mazim, the poet, saith, " Speak well of thyself, for even thy kinsmen will declare thy faults."

At Jaffa, my master fell sick, and calling me to his bedside, he said, "Abel, I like not strangers. Abide with me and thy reward shall be great."

Then I fell upon my knees, and swore, by the ruby in his bosom, to stay with him night and day till he bade me go.

" Oh, my master," said I, " I will watch thee with the eyes of the lynx, and touch thee with the hand of thy mother, I will move about thy chamber on panther's feet, and guard thee as she guards her young. To those who love thee, I will be softer than the fur upon her back ; to him that would harm thee, deadlier than her teeth and claws."

In this sore sickness, which lasted many weeks, my master cast out his old disease, and grew day by day into a strong and healthy man.

" Abel," said he, " it is now a long time since I left my father's house, and my heart yearns to see my brethren. To-morrow, a ship will sail for England. We will embark for that country, and visit Egypt at another time."

"The words of my master are wise," said I, "for a man's kindred may pass away, but the Pyramids will endure."

So on the morrow we embarked, and in twenty days entered the greatest city in Frangistan—London.

Wonderful city ! the stores whereof are filled with the riches of the universe ! The shops are on either side of you, and form the greatest bazaar in the world. At first I thought it was all bazaar, for if the shops of London were placed in a row, they would reach from Dan to Beersheba.

As I stood on a great bridge that crosses the river, I saw the ships that brought this merchandise from all climes under the sun. The masts thereof were like a forest of pines on the heights of Mount Lebanon. Over this bridge the people pass and repass for ever and ever. "These English," said I, "know much, but they know not rest. Like the messengers of Abdul the Omnipotent, that look not to the right hand nor to the left, they hurry past you and speak not, having no time for meditation and prayer."

Day by day, I looked into those crowded streets, hoping to see some one fall down upon his knees and pray to the Most High; but I looked and waited in vain. Then came to my mind the word of Ahmed the sage, "The nation that knows not God shall become the prey of devils, and perish utterly." Afterwards, however, I was told that the English believed in God, whom, strange to say, they worship only one day in seven. Once, on what they call the Sabbath Day, I went with my master to one of their mosques to see their mode of worship. The priest was dressed in a long white robe, like one of the mountebanks of Cairo, and while he spake to the people they bowed their heads and groaned. Suddenly, from a recess or gallery in the temple, there came a noise terrible as the howling of wolves at midnight, then awful and deep as the roar of the Jordan, then soft and faint, and far off, like the whisper of the wind through the groves of Mount Olivet. At the first alarm all the people stood up and shouted, and ceased not till the awful sounds were silenced. Looking towards the place whence the noise proceeded, I saw a man making frantic movements with his hands and feet like one possessed with a devil. This fellow, doubtless, was hired by the priest to keep the people in awe with his bellowings. At their religious festivals the idolaters of Hindostan make similar noises with gongs and drums and trumpets. Blessed art thou, and blessed for ever shalt thou be, O Mohammed! for thou hast taught us to worship the One, the only God, without companion, wife, or son.

In various parts of the city I saw many magnificent buildings which, at first, I thought were temples, for I saw the people going in and coming out continually, and from the open doors thereof came a strange odour as of incense. The people that went in and came out were ragged as the beggars that sit at the gates of Aleppo; so I communed with myself, saying "These be the churches of the poor;" but I discovered afterwards that in these temples were sold waters of madness. In England, the ruler of every large city hath many servants clothed in blue, and girt about the loins with a leathern girdle, whose business it is to save the people from the fury of those who have drunk of the enchanted cup. When these madmen are brought to the Hall of Justice, the ruler saith to the rich among them, "Pay so much and begone;" to the poor, who cannot pay, he saith "Away to prison." Such, O my brethren, is the justice of unbelievers; such the condition of this people—a people that knows not God, and despises the commandment of his Prophet.

When my master had tarried a month in London, we journeyed to Manchester. Besides the mosques and the palaces for the sale of strange waters, there are in that city other buildings the dimensions of which are great. These are the cotton factories, for which the place is famous. In some of these one man will employ as many as three thousand slaves, of both sexes and of all ages. Here, they count it as nothing that men and women should mingle together. Among all ranks modesty is unknown. Ladies will sit, even in theatres, with their faces and bosoms uncovered, and they blush not when they stand before you naked as the dancing girls of Egypt.

When my master visited one of these places, he took me with him. The lord of the mill showed us the wonders of the place. Near us was a young maiden watching two machines. Her movements were like those of her shuttles, swifter than the feet of the wild ass.

"Behold," said the lord of the mill, "this slender girl can clothe one thousand women in a week, and the women of Manchester can clothe the women of the world."

After sunset I walked into the city, and turning aside from the streets of palaces I fell among the habitations of the poor. Behold! the women that clothed the world were themselves clad in filthy and miserable rags. There I saw the son despise the father; the daughter set at nought her mother. Little ones were running hither and thither with small vessels containing the waters that make them mad, while everywhere from the open doors came the odour of swine's flesh. Then I cried aloud, "O Ida! fairest maiden of Aleppo! when I see thee arrayed in the tinted garments woven in this city, I know that these wretched and fallen unbelievers were born but to minister to such as thou."

The poor Syrian goes out to his field or his vineyard, and brings the fruit of his toil to the hidden jewel in whom his soul delights; but here the husband drives out his wife to the factory, and riots on her wages. The wolf that famishes among the stones of the desert warms and nourishes her young, but the infidels of this country send out their little ones to earn bread for their parents. Verily the English are a people whom God hath smitten with blindness. Their country is green and beautiful as the meadows of Abana, yet the people live half-buried in narrow and pestilent streets. Their skies are blackened with the smoke of factories and furnaces; their streams poisoned with deadly and abominable things. The poor pile up riches which they dare not touch; the rich live in the midst of a poverty which they fear and hate.

When I saw this my heart grew sick, and I sought my master.

"O my master," I said, "be not angry, I pray thee, with thy servant, but my heart hungers for my native land. Give me the ruby which hath touched the sacred stone at Mecca, and let me go." Then the young lord, my master, paid me my full wages, and heaping many gifts upon me, bade me return to my own land.

GLOSSARY OF LOCAL WORDS.

By W. G. Hird.

INTRODUCTORY OBSERVATIONS.

The word *Dialect* properly means the peculiar words, or forms of speech, which characterise a locality, and are often so marked as to be readily known from those used in other places, and ordinary English. All our large towns in Yorkshire, and many different parts of the rural districts, have their own stock of words, so unlike each other as to be hardly intelligible to persons residing a few miles off. And the varied spelling and pronunciation of the same words in different places is amply sufficient to bewilder strangers. The lofty epithet, "YORKSHIRE DIALECT," applied to any locality in our great county, is both a misnomer and an absurdity, as has been well illustrated by the author of the Leeds Dialect (pp. 8—25) in some happily chosen examples of the different way of speaking in various places at short distances from the centre of our woollen manufactures. The same may be said equally of Bradford and Halifax, and the neighbourhood. Instead of the words in the Dialect Poems being *provincial*, they can only be considered *local*, with but few exceptions, and the words introduced by strangers.

The very uncouth and varied forms of some words may be traced to laziness and imperfect articulation originally, and these have been perpetuated through ignorance. For instance, those beginning with *c* and *g* change the initial letter, as *tlay*, for *clay* ; *dlad* for *glad* ; and the lengthening of monosyllables like *no* and *so* into *noa* and *soa* for the sake of making a mouthful, are sheer remnants of vulgarity. Mr. S. Dyer says, in the *Yorkshire Magazine* (Vol. II., p. 254), that " AWTHER and NAWTHER are found so written as far back as the twelfth century." Further, that " the modes of pronouncing these words seem to differ in each town of Yorkshire ; " and that he had " heard *neither*, *nyther, nayther,* &c. *Nathor* was the Anglo-Saxon spelling." The change of *l* into *w* for the sake of breadth of sound is common in dialect forms, as *cowd* (cold), *fowk* (folk), *owd* (old), &c. The broad pronunciation of the last word was formerly almost universal in Bradford and the neighbour-hood, and is still used by uneducated persons, but in most parts of Yorkshire and the Northern counties is spelled *aud* or *awd*, and in Scottish, *auld*. It is a very common epithet of familiarity and endearment when prefixed to the words *lad* and *lass*, &c., as in the touching line—" Tha mun gie ma thy hand, *owd lad*," p. 33, and in the tender allusion to Owd Mally, p. 14, l. 3, &c.

It has not been thought necessary to note the halting between the use of the aspirate (*h*) and its omission, or the irregularity of the endings of the compound personal pro-nouns, on account of our limited space. The letter *u* is frequently used instead of *e, o,* and *w*, as *hur* for *her; ut,* p. 23, l. 20, for *hot,* where *h* is dropped and *o* changed to *u* ; and *ul,* p. 36, l. 21, for *will* is a further corrupted form of a short word. Better English, or more correct forms of speaking, would have been out of keeping with the characters delineated.

The DIALECT POEMS are singularly rich in *metaphor* and *simile*, which, by their redundancy, add a force and charm to many passages of great beauty. But grammatical accuracy is a thing utterly unknown. The use of a plural nominative with a verb in the singular, and the converse, are almost universal amongst the persons forming the subjects of the Poems: *e.g.*, p. 2, l. 5—" Yond props is like "— for *are* like; *Ib.*, l. 13—" When wasters lewks " *(look)*; *Ib.*, 23—" Theer's few likes tellin' " (there are few like telling); p. 14, l. 1—" It's a mercy wer feelings gets blunted " (our feelings get blunted). Rhyme is also occasionally made by *good* English rather than dialect sounds of words, as *stile* with *while;* where the vulgar pronunciation of the first word would be *steel*. This is allowable in poetry, and often occurs in Burns' Poems. Our author has not much, if at all, exaggerated the common speech of the persons delineated in his Poems. Occasional coarseness, and the use of terms *tabooed* in good society, arrest the attention more by their expressiveness than propriety, whilst the quaint illustrations and homely metaphors cannot fail to interest and please the most fastidious readers, and convey at the same time wholesome truth and instruction. The great object of the Glossary has been to give the correct meaning of the *dialect* words as used by the author. Many of these are now nearly *obsolete*, or *foreign* to vast numbers of persons who have come to reside here in consequence of the wonderful development and rapid growth of our manufacturing industries. The small country town of half a century ago, with its rural environs so finely described in *Olden Days* (pp. 152-3), has, under the fostering influence of commercial enterprise, increased its population tenfold, and become one of the great centres of our staple manufactures which find employment for thousands and promote the general welfare of the community.

AARNS, page 19, line 3.—A corruption of the Saxon verb *earnian, to gain by labour.* The word also means *to merit,* or *deserve.* The form *arn, to earn,* occurs p. 17, l. 5. It is also common in *Salop.*—(*Halliwell's Dictionary of Archaic Words,* p. 85.)

ABAHT, p. 1, l. 1.—*About.* The letters *ah* are largely used for *ou* in dialect words, *e.g.,* clahd (cloud), hahse (house), mahse (mouse), fahnd (found), pahnd (pound), &c.

ABOON, p. 33, l. 21.—*Above.* " *Yond place aboon,*" *i.e.,* Heaven. The same idea occurs at p. 34, l. 19. The word is also used for the comparative " *more than,*" as " *aboon a bit.*"

ADDLED, p. 24, l. 15.—*Earned.* The same as *adyld.*

ADEN, p. 98, l. 11.—The same as the Hebrew *Eden, delight, pleasure;* the name of the first abode of Adam and Eve.

AHT, p. 6, l. 21.—*Out.* Compare this with ab*ah*t, with*ah*t, and d*ah*t.

AH, p. 2, l. 10.—The personal pronoun *I;* as " *Ah* (I) *sud say.*" This is often prefixed to contractions of *am, have, had, shall,* and *will,* &c., as

AH'M, p. 4, l. 9.—"*Ah'm* (I am) *nut a woman,*" &c. The next line gives the pronoun *I* correctly, as, " *But I can tell,*" &c.

AH'VE, p. 4, l. 21.—"*Ah've* (I have) *bowt* (bought)," &c.; and at p. 33, l. 17, "*Ah've* (I have) *wished 'at ah'd* (that I had)," &c.

AH'LL, p. 4, l. 4.—*I will.* " *Ah'll* (I will) *fotch,*" &c.

AL, p. 3, l. 24.—"*An' al* (and I will) *set t'kettle on.*"

AL BE, p. 33, l. 24.—"*Al be* (will be) *heaven of itseln to me.*"

ALEASS, p. 29, l. 20.—*Alehouse.*

ASS'D, p. 46, l. 12.—*Asked.* A variant of the Saxon verb *axian, to ask or request.* The same as *axed,* p. 6, l. 5. Both forms of this word occur on p. 62, lines 7, 20.

'AT, p. 4, l. 9.—*That.* " *A woman 'at* (that) *oft speyks.*"

AT's, p. 48, l. 12.—*That are.* " *The blaws 'at's* (that are) *intended,*" &c.

AUTHER, p, 29, l. 10.—A coarse form of *Either.* The correspondent of *nauther,* for *neither.*

AWLUS, p. 9, l. 16.—*Always.* Sometimes in the Leeds dialect, *awalus.*

AXED,—See ASS'D.

BAHN, p. 11, l. 11.—*Going.* This is the general signification of the word, but it has several others. Sometimes it includes the idea of *dying,* or *about to die,* as on p. 4, l. 24. It seems to be the same as *Boun* or *Bown, ready,* &c., from the A.S. *abunden,* a word often used by Chaucer. See further Vocabulary of Halifax words in the Appendix to *Hunter's Hallamshire Glossary,* p. 140, London, Pickering, 1829; and the *Dialect of Craven,* vol. I., p. 43, Sec. Ed., London, 1828.

BAHNCING, p. 62, l. 20.—*Bouncing, i.e., Boasting.* From the D. *Bonzen.*

BECOS, p. 49, l. 20.—*Because.* Sometimes contracted to '*Cos.*

BEGOW, p. 23, l. 18.—*An exclamation* or *oath (Leeds Dialect,* p. 261). This is evidently a mere exclamation or harmless expletive with our author, as well as the kindred words, *Egow, Igow,* and *By t'Megs.*

BENG-UP-CHAP, p. 1, l. 7.—A climax for *well-formed and good-looking,* as opposed to *little and decrepit.* In the *Leeds Dialect,* p. 242, the phrase *Bang-up* has at least a dozen different applications and shades of meaning.

BLATIN' CREW, p. 31, l. 10.—*Noisy children.* A rather coarse but common metaphor representing children as a number of sheep *bleating* or *responding* to each other's cries.

BLUTHER, p. 18, l. 16.—*To sob loudly, or make a great noise.* The same as the Craven word *blother.*

BRAH, p. 32, l. 18.—*Brow,* or *top of hill;* p. 16, l. 17, *The forehead.*

BRAT, p. 15, l. 12.—A contemptuous epithet for *Child.*

BREEDIN' HURRIES, p. 7, l. 28.—*Causing disturbances,* or *quarrels.*

BOGGARD, p. 2, l. 16, &c.—*A ghost ; a goblin.* (*Halliwell's Dictionary,* vol. I., p. 191.)

BOWT, p. 4, l. 21.—*Bought.* Compare *rowt* (wrought), p. 37, line 1, for change of vowels *ou* into *ow* for the sake of breadth of sound.

CAAR'D DAHN, p. 43, l. 14.—*Bent down, i.e.,* stooped down. *Caar'd, Car,* and *Cahr* are mere variations in the spelling of the word *Cower,* from the Welsh *Cwrian, to crouch.*

CADGE, p. 35, l. 32.—*To beg importunately.*

CAHNCILD, p. 24, l. 10.—*Properly, counselled. " Counsel, to gain the affections;* he has *counselled* her at last."— (*Craven Dialect,* vol. I., p. 88.) Although metamorphosed in spelling, the old Bradford pronunciation of this word is fairly given.

CAHR, p. 16, l. 1.—*Sit down, rest.* See CAAR'D.

CAPT, p. 6, l. 19.—*Surprised, astonished.*

CARRYIN'S ON, p. 65, l. 17.—*Actions, conduct, proceedings.*

CANNAL, p. 37, l. 8.—*Candle.* In the Craven dialect, *canle.* The termination of several other words in *dle* is similarly changed, as *hannals* (handles), p. 20, l. 1 ; *Spinnal* (spindle), p. 30, l. 23, &c.

'CESS, p. 65, l. 8.—*Assessment, Poor's Rates.*

CHAP, p. 8, l. 13.—*Man ; " A familiar term for a companion."* —(*Halliwell's Dictionary,* p. 240.)

CLAAD, p. 9, l. 22.—*Cloud.* Also spelled CLAHD, p. 31, l. 17.

CLAM, p. 63, l. 20.—*To hunger or starve.* The only sense in which this word is used by our author, although it has several other meanings.

CONSATE, p. 2, l. 9.—*Conceit, fancy, opinion.* SELF-CONSATE, *High opinion of self.*

CONSITHER, p. 23, l. 9.—*Consider, or think well.*

'COS, p. 7, l. 7.—A contraction of *becos* for *because.*

COWDS, p. 5, l. 11.—*Colds.*

DAL, p. 29, l. 2.—An objectionable word formerly much used; perhaps often without any definite idea of its import. It is also common in several other large towns, and has been explained as follows:—" A petty oath." " *Dal* it, whoad a thowt it."—*(Leeds Dialect,* p. 280.)

DEE, p. 4, l. 28.—*Die.*

DEEIN', p. 8, l. 7.—*Dying.*

DENG or DANG, p. 18, l. 32.—A word akin to DAL, said to be the past tense of the Gaelic DING. " *Od dang, or od ding,* a mutilated oath."—*(Craven Dialect,* vol I., p. 100) Halliwell regards it as an imprecation, and says, perhaps it is a softening of *damn,* and very common in the provinces.—*(Dictionary of Archaic Words,* vol. I., p. 291.)

DIDDLED, p. 31, l. 20.—*Deceived, or cheated.* An every-day word in Leeds as well as Bradford: *e.g.,* " *Diddled* mah art o' sixpence." " He's a rum un *to diddle.*" " Doant goa *diddle* t'poor fellah—ah sudn't like it mesen."—*(Leeds Dialect,* p. 282.)

DLAD, p. 33, l. 4.—*Glad.*

DLASS, p. 19, l. 4.—*Glass.*

DLUM, p. 14, l. 3.—*Sad, disconsolate.* This is the exact meaning intended by our author; but, as Hunter says, " to look *glum* is to have a dissatisfied, discontented look; pouting frowning, sullen. It is the same word with *gloom*."—*(Hallamshire Glossary*, p. 44.)

DOLT, p. 2, l. 1.—*A shapeless lump.* This is the obvious meaning, whatever may be the origin of the word. It is also applied jeeringly to a *stupid person, i.e.,* one either *unwilling*, or *incapable of learning matters correctly.*

DOWDY, p. 8, l. 1.—The word denotes here a *scolding, irritable woman*, acting like a spoiled child when not allowed to have her own way in everything. But in its application as an epithet to Sarah Slurr at p. 24, l. 3, the vice of *hypocrisy* is included. The Lancashire word DOWD, according to Halliwell, means "*flat, dead, spiritless.*"—*(Dictionary of Archaic Words, &c.,* vol. l., p. 314.) And DOUDY in the Craven dialect signifies "*a dirty woman. Icelandic* DOUDA, *an idle person.*"—*(Horæ Momentæ Cravenæ*, p. 70. Anon. London, 1824.)

DOWLY, p. 29, l. 19.—*Comfortless.* This word has other meanings according to its application, and has been thus defined: "DOWLY, *melancholy*, from *dule*, sorrow. Welsh, DULYN. French, DEUIL. When *dowly* is applied to a person's look it signifies melancholy, but when applied to situation it means lonely or retired. 'Ye look vara *dowly*.' 'This is a *dowly* place to live at;'" &c.—*(The Dialect of Craven*, vol. l., p. 116.)

DOY, p. 15, l. 1.—*Joy, darling.* A pet word applied to children.

DREE, p. 32, l. 5; p. 45, l. 2.—*Wearisome, tedious.* Here applied to *time*, but often "*to a road*," as remarked by Hunter in his *Hallamshire Glossary*, p. 32.

DRUCKEN, p. 32, l. 6—*Drunken.* Compare *Sucken*, p. 21, l. 9, where a similar change and elision of *n* takes place. *Drucken* was the original spelling of this word in Burns' poem on Scotch Drink, continued even in the Third Ed. of his works.

DUE, p. 5, l. 21; p. 29, l. 8.—*To do.* The Craven form omits the final vowel.

DUFFERS, p. 30, l. 10.—*Mere pretenders* who lack courage when brought to face danger, or difficulty.

EBLIS, p. 134, l. 10.—One of the Arabic names of the *Devil*, signifying the *Calumniator;* thought to have been formed by Mohammed from *balas,* a profligate, wicked person.—*(Rodwell's Translation of the Koran,* Notes, pp. 187, 370.)

EE, p. 46, l. 26.—*Eye.*

EEBREES, p. 41, l. 11.—*Eyebrows.*

EEEMIN', p. 14, l. 7.—*Evening.*

EEN, p. 8, l. 1.—*Eyes.* Sometimes both spelled and pronounced *ees.*

EGOY, p. 2, l. 14.—A petty oath ; but here, a mere exclamation of surprise or wonder. Perhaps the same as BY GOW.—*Leeds Dialect,* p. 261.

ENAH, p. 8, l. 12.—*In a short time.*

EUST, p. 23, l. 7.—*Was accustomed to ; had the habit of.*

FAAS, p. 25, l. 7; p. 32, l. 26.—*Face.* In the Leeds Dialect *fa-ace.* It is also correctly used at p. 50, l. 13, *face,* and rhymes with *place,* l. 15.

FAN, p. 23, l. 17.—*Found.*

FAVER, or FAVVER, p. 2, l. 15.—*Resemble.*

FEHW, p. 8, l. 23.—*Few.* In the Leeds Dialect *faew.*

FESHUN, p. 15, l. 10.—In this place, " hardly could feshun " means felt so ashamed that she scarcely durst or had the courage to look out ; but at p. 30, l. 18, it signifies *style of dress, gay or fine clothing.*

FEYT, p. 29, l. 2.—*Fight, i.e.,* struggle bravely for the right.

FLAWPIN, p. 23, l. 6.—Same as " FLOPING, coming in with a dash, but with an implication of the ridiculous ; also, *flirting, with the same sense,*"—*(Leeds Dialect,* p. 205.) Halliwell says *Flawps* means—" an awkward, noisy, untidy, and slovenly person."—*(Dictionary,* p. 361.)

FLAYED, p. 25, l. 22 ; p. 46, l. 32.—*Afraid ; frightened.* In Burns' " Halloween," l. 184, this word occurs as *fleyd,* and is explained in Currie's note, *scared, frighted.*

FLEER, p. 26, l. 18.—*To laugh,* or *sneer wantonly.*

FORRAD, p. 3, l. 23.—*Forward.* The same in several dialects.

FRAME, p. 35, l. 3.—*Begin ; get ready.*

GAAT, p. 23, l. 4.—*The door, or framed bars* used for closing the entrance to a walled city, road, or enclosure. CREAKIN' GAAT, literally, *one nearly worn out and making a noise when used :* hence, figuratively, a person in apparently very poor health, or in almost dying circumstances.

GATE, p. 16, l. 4.—*Way, i.e.* dead ; as, *tha wor weel aht o' t'gate;* p. 30, l. 22 : "*Get aht o' t'gate*" [the way]. Hunter says the *gate* is the *highroad.* A *gate* opening into a field is a *yate.* A *gate* of a city is a *bar;* as Micklegate bar at York, the bar of the great street [Roman road].—*(Hallamshire Glossary,* p. 42.) GATE, p. 27, l. 17, *Got.* The past tense of the verb *get.*

GERNIN', p. 32, l. 3.—*Grinning ; snarling.*

GIRDS, p. 8, l. 28.—*Spasms; fits ; sudden and violent pains.*

GIRDS (for GIRDLES), p. 56, l. 1.—*Binds,* or *surrounds.*

GIRN, p. 26, l. 18.—*A scornful grin,* or *laugh.*

GOBBLE UP, p. 19, l. 5.—*Eat greedily.*

GLOARS, p. 3, l. 28.—*Stares hard.* Also spelled *glore* and *glower.*

GRONNY, p. 15, l. 1.—Rather *Granny*, *i.e.*, *grandmother.* In Cumberland, *grondy.*

HAAR, p. 47, l. 3.—*Hour.* " *This awf haar* [hour] *ur near.*"

HAASEL GOOIDS, p. 27, l. 13. — *Household Goods*, *i.e.*, furniture.

HAHR, p. 25, l. 2.—*Hour.* The *h* is omitted p. 6, l. 15, *e.g.*, " *To ivvery ahr*," &c.

HAHSE, p. 5, l. 1.—*House.* The plural *hahsuz* occurs, p. 34, l. 11, &c.

HAL, p. 41, l. 24.—Perhaps, a contraction of *hallabaloo*, *uproar*, or *confused noise.*

HALS, p. 32, l. 7.—*Fools.*

HAY-BAY, p. 44, l. 20.—*A noisy* or *derisive laugh.* In the Leeds Dialect, *ha-ba*, pronounced *ha-a ba-a* (p. 318).

HECTORED, p. 30, l. 10.—*Bullied.* From HECTOR, the name of a famous Trojan leader.

HING, p. 5, l. 27.—*Hang.* An old form of the verb in use before the time of the Reformation.— *(Hunter's Glossary, p. 49.)*

HOIL, p. 65, l. 5.—A slang name for the *Lock-up* or *Cell* in which persons are placed before trial. Perhaps there is some allusion to those miserable *cellars* or *dungeons* formerly used for *prisons*, which deserved no better name. For example, " *The Black Hole* " at Calcutta.

HOIN, p. 39, l. 15.—*To ill-use* or *treat unmercifully*, as explained by the allusion to the cruel sport of school boys stoning frogs and toads; typifying the hard struggle of Poll Blossom's parents to obtain a livelihood. " 'This may possibly come from the A.S. *hine, a servant*, who was put to great hardships in doing his lord's work," &c.—*(Appendix to Hunter's Glossary, p. 150.)*

Hur, p. 24, l. 12.—*Her.* The form of the pronoun here given occurs thirteen times in "T'Creakin' Gaat," but in most instances elsewhere is correctly spelled.

Jock, p. 3, l. 28.—*Food,* or *Meals.*

Karkiss, p. 3, l. 4.—*Carcase, i.e., body,* or *bodily appearance.*
Kests, p. 2, l. 21.—*Casts,* or *throws,* as—*Kests* [casts] *a leet.*
Kuss, p. 46, l. 24.—*Kiss.* "*Nor offered to give ma a kuss.*"

Leet, p. 2, l. 21.—*A Light.* Leetid, p. 19, l. 16, *Lighted.*
Lewkt, p. 4, l. 13.—*Looked,* or *appeared.*
Lug, p. 1, l. 12.—*To pull the hair,* or *ears. Lug* is also used for the *ear,* and *handle of a jug;* as " pool his *lugs*" [ears] ; " bring t'pitcher by *t'lug* " [handle].

Madlin', p. 2, l. 3.—A rather useful word amongst illiterate persons, both in its *noun* and *verbal* meanings. " A *madling* acts in opposition to common sense. He is an *owd madling* whose reason has become childish by the lapse of years. *To be madling* is to have our ideas confused. Untoward events may rapidly overtake a man, so that from their force he becomes absent-minded, or *maddled,* at times ; or more to the letter of our word, comes to be *madling,* or thinking about what he ought not to think about then."—*(Leeds Dialect,* pp. 354-5.) Hunter says Maddle is the old word *to meddle,* in its sense of to mix, to confuse. Fr. *mele.*—*(Glossary,* p. 63.)
Mebbe, p. 6, l. 27.—*Perhaps,* or *possibly.* Same as *may-be,* or *it may be,* and the Craven *mebby, i.e., probably.*
Meet, p. 2, l. 11.—*Might, strength.*
Megs, p. 2, l. 6.—*By t'Megs.* Supposed to mean by *St. Margaret;* a kind of oath.—*(Craven Dialect,* vol. I., p. 317.)

MESHT, p. 3, l. 1.—Literally, *smashed, broken in pieces;* figuratively, in this place, *impaired in mind and body through the fall.*

MICHAEL, p. 35, l. 3.—The archangel represented by Milton as the leader of the hosts of heaven against Satan is here invoked, instead of Apollo, to inspire him whilst composing a song, when engaged on other singular business. The piece throughout deeply commiserates the condition of the poor Lancashire operatives, and exhibits at the same time a curious mixture of drollery and satire, which rendered it popular; and the sale, according to Mr. A. Holroyd, realised a trifle towards the relief of the distressed factory workers.

MOOILD AN' TEW, p. 4, l. 19.—*Hard labour; continuous toil.* Words of allied meaning used together for the sake of emphasis. The verb *moil,* as explained by Halliwell, is generally coupled with toil, as we *moil* and *toil.—(Dictionary,* p. 558.)

MOULD, p. 1, l. 6.—*Model; pattern.*

MUD, p. 35, l. 5.—*Must; Ib.,* l. 21, *Could, i.e.,* would sacrifice her own life to save the child, *if she cou'd,* from the force of maternal love.

MULE-HOIL, p. 30, l. 24.—The common name of the room in a mill where *weft* is spun by machines called *Mules.* But here, the House of Commons is meant, as may be seen from the banter indulged in at the expense of some of our political leaders.

NAFF, p. 23, l. 16.—*Nave, i.e.,* centre of a wheel, meaning *to sink deeply in sin,* like the wheels of an overladen cart or waggon in the mire.

NAGUEIN', NENGIN' TURN, p. 3, l. 15.—Alliterative words of nearly the same general signification, used intensively. *Gnawing*, from the Anglo-Saxon *gnagan*, used as a descriptive term for an *irritable scold*, or a *constant source of annoyance*, affords a fair explanation of the first word as used by our author. It is even probable that the second is a mere variation of the first word. Besides, according to Halliwell, *gnag, knag*, and *knaggy* are almost similarly used in *Lincolnshire.—(Dictionary*, vol. I., p. 405; II., p. 497.) In the *Leeds Dialect* (p. 371) the first word is spelled *naig*, and pronounced *na-ag*; and several slightly different applications and meanings are also noted.

NAUTHER, p. 31, l. 16.—*Neither*. See Introductory observations, p. 243.

NAVVY, p. 7, l. 3.—*Canal*.

NOBBUD, or NOBBUT, p. 12, l. 4.—*Only; except ; none but.* Or perhaps, when strictly used, *nobbud* means *only* as applied to things ; and *nobbut*, when used of persons, *none but*.

NONCATE, p. 4, l. 1.—A nondescript word for *a silly person.* As *Nont* and *Nuncle* are still sometimes used for *Aunt* and *Uncle*, the word *Noncate* may have been formed from *Aunt Kate*, not in the actual sense of a relation, or the name of a real person, but a *foolish, unmanly,* or *thoughtless individual*.

NOWT, p. 1, l. 9.—*Nothing*.

NUNK, p. 61, l. 1.—*Uncle*.

OD, ROT IT ! p. 7, l. 12.—*Passionate rebuke or remonstrance.* An expression that admits of no defence. It is characteristic under the circumstances, or a faithful transcript of life in one of its lowest phases, which is all that can be said in its extenuation. The author of the Craven Dialect, (vol. II., pp. 15, 16) strongly condemns this and all similar expressions.

OWD DUCKFOOIT, p. 37, l. 11.—An epithet or phrase given by way of pleasant banter to his wife by the old waller, on account of her *not being so nimble as when young*. Their fond attachment to each other in what follows shows that nothing ill-natured was intended or felt on either side.

OWD LAD, p. 33, l. 2.—Words of *great tenderness and affection* here, not the ordinary or contemptuous way in which the word *old* is applied in most instances.

OWD LASS, p. 14, l. 3.—*Old woman.* Spoken in pity, and with affectionate regard. Nearly the same as the sentiment above.

PAHND, p. 61, l. 9; p. 63, l. 12.—*Pound, i.e.,* money : *Pund,* p. 64, l. 24, *Pound* weight.

PAIRTED, p. 12, l. 17.—*Parted.* Sometimes *pa-arted.*

PEARKT, p. 64, l. 1. — *Peaked,* or *perched, examined* or *scrutinised.* An allusion to the way in which cloth is examined by passing it over a roller opposite the light, so as to observe the defects and fine the weavers for bad work.

PESHT, p. 42, l. 18.—*Pushed violently down. Pashd* is also common.

PIT-PATTIN', p. 11, l. 4.—Words imitating the sound of little feet in walking.

PLAT, p. 8, l. 16. —*The floor, or ground.* Also anything *flat.*

POOL, p. 1, l. 11.—*Pull.* To pull the nose, an act of derision and defiance.

POBS, p. 31, l. 2.—A Craven word for *porridge.* Seldom if ever heard in Bradford, except for children's food. It is therefore the language of nurses, not men, and seems out of place here.

POYT, p. 59, l. 12.—" *A poker,* generally the *fire-poit.*"— (*Craven Dialect,* vol. II., p. 52.)

PUDSA DOAS, p. 2, l. 2.—*Pudsey Joe.* A fat, dirty imbecile from Pudsey, who for many years was often seen wandering about the streets of Bradford, and sometimes subjected to coarse practical jokes, which he occasionally avenged on passers-by.

PUFFT, p. 37, l. 4.—*Puffed.* D., *pof,* gently blown away by the wind, or breath. In Burns' *Halloween* this word is spelled *fuff't,* and applied to blowing the smoke out of the mouth.

RAKIN', p. 6, l. 21.—*Rambling out late at nights for pleasure or amusement.*

REYT, p. 1, l. 5.—*Right.* A word usually denoting excellence in compounds, as *dahnreyt, upreyt.*

ROARED, p. 8, l. 3.—*Wept passionately and made a great noise.* But sometimes both the verb and the participle *roarin'* are used for *weeping* only.

RUMMIST, p. 65, l. 17.—*Strangest; most ludicrous.*

SAMM'D, p. 39, l. 14.—*Gathered; collected.*

SAUKIN', p. 35, l. 23.—*Sucking.* In *Halliwell's Dictionary* (p. 775) the verb is spelled *souke,* and said to be Anglo-Norman.

SCAR, p. 5, l. 23.—*Scour.*

SCRAN, p. 36, l. 18.—*Food.*

SCRAWK, p. 41, l. 2.—*A stroke,* or only part of a letter.

SHUTTERED, p. 8, l. 8.—*Slipped out.*

SKRIKIN', p. 41, l. 27.—*Shrieking, screaming.*

SHOO, p. 4, l. 7.—*She.* The Yorkshire equivalent of the Lancashire and Derbyshire *hoo.* Anglo-Saxon, *heo.*

SLARIN' WIFE, p. 24, l. 21.—*Lazy and dirty.* A pretender only to cleanliness, who left the dirt on, and neglected all that could be passed unobserved.

SLOPER LOIN, p. 27, l. 15.—*Sloper Lane,* a slang phrase for

S

the *sly way* in which persons disappear from a place after having cheated or deceived shopkeepers and all who have trusted them.

SNUFF, p. 37, l. 8.—*Ashes of the burnt wick.*

SOMEHAH, p. 2, l. 21.—*Somehow, in some way.*

SPINE I' T'BACK, p. 5, l. 11.—A redundant phrase, curiously applied to *any affection of the spine.*

STATTY, p. 1, l. 3.—*A statue.*

SUD, p. 2, l. 10.—A contraction of *should; Suddant*, p. 6, l. 3, *should not.* Compare *wod* and *woddant.*

SUMMAT, p. 2, l. 28.—*Something.*

SWEALED, p. 37, l. 8. — A metaphor implying that old Moxy's life had been prematurely shortened by poor food and hard labour, as a candle is wasted by a current of air on one side. "Fotch a shool-ful o' round coil [*i.e.* little lumps, —no small coal or smudge] an' mind an' doan't *sweal* t'cannel."—*(Leeds Dialect,* p. 425.)

TA, p. 11, l. 11,—A contraction of *tha, thou.* But at p. 41, l. 11, *ta* seems to have a tinge of scorn not found in the familiar *thou.*

TEMM'D, p. 37, l. 18.—*Poured*, from the word *teem.* "This was good usage in the time of Elizabeth."—*(Hunter's Glossary*, p. 88.)

TENGED, p. 42, l. 2.—*Stung, enraged. Teng*, for the *sting* of a wasp or bee, and also as a verb, was formerly very common in Bradford.

TENGIN', p. 5, l. 10.—*Stinging.*

TENGS, p. 2, l. 6.—*Tongs.*

TEW, p. 5, l. 15.—*Strive or work hard.* See *Tug* and *Mooild* and *Tew.* "Taews hard for a living. Nah just sea bud! Nobbud to luke here! Ye may rive an'-tug-an'-taew an' yuh can't hardly brek em," says a vendor of bootlaces accustomed to hold forth in the market place."—(*Leeds Dialect*, p. 433.)

TEWIN', p. 27, l. 25.—*Hard-working.*

THA, p. 8, l. 27.—*Thou.*

THAH'S, p. 9, l. 14.—*Thou hast.*

THOIL, p. 11, l. 20.—*Afford.* Only one of the several meanings given to this word according to its application. To thoil is to be generous, and to have no thoil, means intensely selfish. It is also spelled *thoyl.*

THOWT, p. 1, l. 3.—*Thought.* Most words ending in *ought*, in the dialect forms assume the broader sound and spelling *owt*, as bowt (bought), nowt (nought), wrowt (wrought), &c.

TIFT, p. 41, l. 18.—*A fit of scorn, rage, or resentment.*

TLAMM'D, p. 34, l. 12.—*Clammed, starved, wanted food.*

TLAY, p. 22, l. 13.—*Clay.* See introductory observations.

TLEAR, p. 1, l. 4.—*Clear.*

TLOAS, p. 25, l. 12.—*Clothes.*

TLOIS, p. 64, l. 1.—*Close.* This word is spelled *cloise*, p. 224, l. 9.

TLUTHERED, p. 60, l. 9.—*Cluthered, i.e.,* crowded round.

TONTS, p. 42, l. 1.—*Taunts, jeers, or reproaches.*

TRASH or TRESH, p. 9, l. 20.—*Anything worthless* ; here a term of bitter resentment by Natterin' Nan to an imaginary successor. The word is also given to a wanton female who goes out at nights to tempt others. The adjective *trashy* means *worthless*, and the verb *to walk till weary* ; hence

TRESHIN', p. 6, l. 16.—*Walking out and in till weary, or tired out.*

TREYD, p. 19, l. 1.—*Tread, trample on ; i.e., ill-use.*

TUG AN' TEW, p. 5, l. 15.—*Work hard and strive.* Words of nearly the same signification, coupled for the sake of emphasis. Tug means primarily *to tow* or *drag a boat on a canal*, and secondarily, *great physical exertion :* Tew, *continuous, or exhaustive labour.*

Wake, p. 7, l. 7.—*Weak in body, and dejected in mind.* Wakely, p. 38, l. 3, *weakly.*

Wah! Wah! p. 2, l. 25.—*Well! Well!*

Wahr, p. 16, l. 2.—*Worse.*

Wasters, p. 2, l. 13.—The name given to imperfect articles of cutlery sold at a less price by hardware manufacturers. The same word is applied by iron and brass founders to defective castings. Hence, when the epithet *wasters* is given to persons it denotes *want of intellect, stupidity,* or *ignorance.* In some parts of Lancashire *waistril* signifies a *vile* or *worthless person.*

Weel, p. 4, l. 16.—*Well, in good health.*

Weg, or Wag, p. 5, l. 19.—*Move*, literally; but, *help* or *render assistance* in household work is what is meant.

We'se, p. 2, l. 28.—*We shall,* as " *We'se fynd a summat wreng.*"

We'se, p. 2, l. 11.—*We should.* " *We'se hate wursen,*" &c.

Whewin', p. 6, l. 10.—*Whistling of the wind, or making a loud noise in its passage through a small opening.*

Whittle, p. 6, l. 12.—*A large knife.*

Whol, p. 5, l. 16.—*While.*

Whot, p. 4, l. 17.—*What.*

Wisht, or rather Whisht, p. 33, l. 15.—*Hushed, silent; i.e.,* the rest of the family having gone to bed and asleep. In the *Leeds Dialect,* p. 448, the word is further explained : " *Silent, a command to silence.*" " As whisht as a mahs." " Whisht, barns! t'babby's asleep."

Witta, p. 4, l. 1.—An abbreviation of *Will thou.*

WIZAND, p. 12, l. 13 ; p. 32, l. 16.—*Withered ; shrunk ; old looking.*

WOD, p. 9, l. 4.—*Would.*

WODDANT, p. 5, l. 19.—*Would not.*

WOR, p. 6, l. 3.—*Was.*

WUR, p. 2, l. 11.—*Our ; Ib.* WURSEN, *ourselves.*

WURRIT, p. 3, l. 20.—*One always complaining.* An epithet perhaps derived from the verb *to worry.* The word is common to several dialects, in the sense of *to teaze ; to worry,* &c. "Wurrited to death, what one thing an' what another." " God help them 'at hes barns, says I, fur wurrit, wurrit, wurrit, thu'd wurrit a body's life out on 'em."—*(Leeds Dialect,* p. 453.)

ADDENDA.

RALPH GOODWIN, (pp. 107, 8).—The *nom de plume* of
JAMES WADDINGTON, of Saltaire, has been retained by our
author, probably out of affection for the memory of his friend
and the happy significance of the latter part.   Mr. Abraham
Holroyd, to whom JAMES WADDINGTON was intimately
known, gave an affecting account of his life, disposition,
attainments, and characteristic modesty, in *The Bradfordian*
for December, 1861, with the Poem on his death.   This was
a heart-felt tribute of respect for the deceased, and followed
by some beautiful lines by a Bradford *Mœcenas* who has
often sympathised with and assisted poor authors in their
struggles for existence.   No apology is needed for their
introduction here, as they breathe the true spirit of poetry,
and finely pourtray WADDINGTON'S *outward* and *inner life.*

> Gentle in word and deed thy life has been ;
> By Nature taught without, and grace within.
> A scholar meek and apt, thou learn'dst in time,
> While yet a youth, to live the life sublime ;
> And now the Poet and the Christian soar,
> In worlds of light, while we thy loss deplore.

This was the introduction to the Elegy on RALPH GOODWIN,
which has been justly considered one of the finest in the
language, for chaste and elegant diction, as well as true
Christian sentiment.

www.ingramcontent.com/pod-product-compliance
Lightning Source LLC
Chambersburg PA
CBHW021100030726
47496CB00006B/1920